★

"You brought Judy Porter to the morgue to identify him."

"Right. She zeroed in on the wedding ring he was wearing. It matched hers and she passed out. Not that I blame the poor girl. His appearance is going to give me nightmares."

Dana let out a deep breath and sat down in the nearest chair. "Do you think it was an accidental drowning?"

"Maybe."

"Do you suspect foul play?" Dana asked urgently.

"Maybe."

"Bruno, you've been working homicide long enough to look at the victim and the circumstances of the case and have an educated opinion. What is it in this case?"

"Off the record?"

"Of course," she promised.

"My educated guess is that someone beat the life out of him and dumped him in the lake, probably off the Manheim Bridge where the water is too deep to freeze."

★

Previously published Worldwide Mystery title by
CAROL COSTA

A DEADLY HAND

THE MASTER PLAN
CAROL COSTA

W⬤RLDWIDE.

TORONTO • NEW YORK • LONDON
AMSTERDAM • PARIS • SYDNEY • HAMBURG
STOCKHOLM • ATHENS • TOKYO • MILAN
MADRID • WARSAW • BUDAPEST • AUCKLAND

For my grandchildren, Angela Ann, Joseph Robert,
Michael Riley, Catherine Ryan, Justine Annette and
Anthony James, who fill my life with joy.

Recycling programs
for this product may
not exist in your area.

THE MASTER PLAN

A Worldwide Mystery/April 2011

First published by Avalon Books

ISBN-13: 978-0-373-26748-4

Copyright © 2009 by Carol Costa

Acknowledgments

Thanks to my husband, Frank, for his patience and willingness to let me talk through my ideas on plotting and characters.

Thanks to my agents, Andree Abecassis and Lettie Lee at the Ann Elmo Agency.

Thanks to all my friends in The Society of Southwestern Authors for their support and inspiration.

ONE

"I'M GETTING MARRIED," Casey said breathlessly. She held out her left hand to show the glittering diamond on her ring finger. "I'm sorry, Dana. I just couldn't hold it in any longer."

It was Monday afternoon and the weekly staff meeting at Globe Investigations was taking place in Dana Sloan's office. Dana, her secretary, Marianne, and two other investigators, Casey Jordan and Bob Farrell, had been discussing a new case involving an auto-repair garage that had recently opened in Crescent Hills.

Globe Investigations had received several letters of complaint about the garage, stating that when a car was brought in for maintenance or repairs, the garage called the owners and reported that the vehicles needed major work done, and then charged the owners exorbitant prices to fix the cars. They had just agreed that Casey would bring a car to the garage for an oil change and see what transpired.

"Does that mean you're going to stick me with the garage gig?" Bob asked Casey with a grin.

Marianne was already on her feet, enthusiastically hugging Casey. "When did this happen? I didn't even know you were seeing someone."

"I'm just kidding, Casey," Bob said as he lifted himself carefully from the chair he had managed to squeeze his plump body into when the meeting began. "Congratulations."

"You're not supposed to say congratulations to the bride," Marianne told him. "That's what you say to the groom."

"Okay. Where is he? Is he someone we know?"

"No," Casey replied. "His name is Tony Hunter. I met him on the golf course at the Crescent Hills Country Club."

"How did you get in there?" Bob asked. "That's where the rich folk play."

"I had a bit of a windfall and I used it to join the Country Club a few months ago." Casey looked at her coworkers and smiled weakly.

"It must have been some windfall to get you accepted into that snob haven," Bob persisted. "Well, I'm happy for you, kid. Whoever he is, Tony Hunter is a lucky man."

"He sure is," Marianne agreed. "And you are going to be a beautiful bride."

"You will keep helping me?" Casey asked Marianne. "Tony probably wouldn't have looked at me twice if you hadn't taken me under your wing."

"Oh, wow," Marianne said, her lovely green eyes sparkling with excitement. "Can I help you with your hair and makeup for the wedding?"

Casey nodded.

Marianne was the resident beauty expert, mostly because she was a gorgeous young woman with wavy auburn hair and a face and figure that stopped traffic. Fortunately for the staff at Globe Investigations, Marianne was as smart and efficient as she was beautiful, and they all admitted she made the office run like a well-oiled machine.

Before Marianne and her hairdresser had worked their magic on Casey, the investigator had never bothered to try and enhance her attractive features with makeup or clothes that actually complemented her tall, slim frame. Casey had worn her dull brown hair long, letting it hang straight or pulling it back into a ponytail. Her normal attire consisted of jeans and T-shirts in the summer, and jeans and sweatshirts in the winter.

Now Casey's hair was highlighted with blond streaks and cut short so that it framed her face and made it look fuller. Her eyeglasses had been replaced by contact lenses and the expert use of mascara and eye shadow had made them her most outstanding feature. She still refused to use standard lipstick, but Marianne had showed her how to use a light blush on her cheeks and a lip gloss that had only the slightest hint of color.

The jeans and baggy shirts had disappeared. Casey wore skirts and slacks with matching jackets and blouses that gave her a chic, professional appearance.

"You already had the looks," Marianne said proudly. "We just helped you make the most of them."

"Uh-oh," Bob complained. "If you gals are going to start discussing makeup and hairdos, I'm leaving."

Dana, who had been strangely silent, finally rose from her chair and walked over to Casey. "I'm very happy for you, Casey," she said as she embraced her.

"Thanks, Dana. I think I've got it all worked out now."

"I hope so," Dana said softly.

"What does that mean?" Bob asked.

"Nothing you have to worry about, Bob," Dana said. "Well, I've got to meet with Sam in a few minutes, so I guess I'd better adjourn this meeting. Both of you have assignments for the next few days, so we'll just meet again on Thursday afternoon for reports and any new cases that come in."

Dana headed for the door and everyone else prepared to follow her out. Marianne and Casey were chattering away about weddings in general, and Bob was using the phone to call his wife. Dana opened the door to the hallway and walked to the elevator.

Dana Sloan had been working for the *Globe* newspaper in Crescent Hills, Illinois, since graduating from college with a degree in journalism. Her talent for digging below the surface of a story and uncovering facts often overlooked by other reporters had soon come to the attention of the *Globe*'s managing editor, Sam McGowan.

Within a few years, Dana was moved from a tiny cubicle in the newsroom to her own office. From there she moved into her current position as the lead investigator and supervisor of Globe Investigations.

Crescent Hills was a growing, prosperous community about fifty miles from Chicago. Sam McGowan believed that a town's primary newspaper should do more than report the news and social events; it should service its community by listening to problems and trying to find solutions. Sam had expanded his desire to help Crescent Hills residents into a separate investigative office supported by the newspaper. Over the years, Dana and her staff had answered the thousands of calls for help that came in daily by way of telephone, regular mail and e-mail.

When readers reported businesses like the garage that was suddenly discovering costly repairs, Dana or one of her staff investigated the allegations and either proved them right or dismissed them.

While Globe Investigations tried not to interfere in police matters, sometimes Dana and her staff's efforts to help their clients led them into the midst of a serious crime. As Crescent Hills grew in population, so did the reports of murder, kidnapping and armed robbery. There had been several occasions when Dana's efforts had uncovered crucial evidence or leads in criminal cases.

A recent investigation had pitted Dana against a corrupt politician and pushed her into the path of a deranged serial killer. That same case had also caused a serious rift in Dana's relationship with Homicide Detective Al Bruno.

Bruno thought that lovely young women like Dana should not be sleuths. He wanted the thoughts under Dana's light brown curls to be about marriage and babies. He wanted Dana to use her intelligence and quick wit to plan menus and parent-teacher events. Although Dana admitted that she loved Al Bruno and would probably marry him someday, she was not ready to give up her career for him. She liked working for Globe Investigations and relished the excitement of working on the cases brought to her attention by the reading public.

Dana and Bruno had formed a recent truce and were supposed to be working on building a stronger relationship. Both of them knew that it was just a matter of time before another case came along that would cause more problems in their romance, but in the meantime they were trying to concentrate on the things that had brought them together rather than the things that pulled them apart.

As the elevator deposited Dana on the second floor of the building where the newsroom and the managing editor's office were located, Dana's thoughts had already settled on the next conflict between herself and Bruno. When she told him that Casey was getting married, Dana was sure Bruno would be upset. After all, Casey had only known Tony Hunter for a few months, while Dana and Bruno had been together for more than two years.

It was after four and the newsroom was quieter than usual. The evening edition was already rolling off the press, so the newsroom staff had wound down. Some of the reporters were out on the streets looking for headline events to include in the early-morning edition. Others were working on the columns and less newsworthy items that would also appear in the morning paper.

12 THE MASTER PLAN

Dana made her way across the room toward Sam's office. A number of people called out greetings and waved to her, but Dana was already late for her meeting and didn't stop to chat.

"Sorry I'm late," Dana apologized as soon as she entered the office. "Casey announced her engagement in the middle of our staff meeting."

"Really?" Sam's bushy gray eyebrows rose slightly. "I thought she was going to dump that guy?"

"I thought so too, but she told me they worked things out. And she's got a lovely diamond on her finger to prove it."

"You don't sound happy for her."

Dana sat down in one of the leather chairs facing Sam's desk. "I'll be happy when I'm sure she's going to be happy."

Sam nodded. "Are you going to tell Bruno?"

"Actually, I'm going to ask him to check this guy out. Casey asked me to help her do that right after they started dating, but neither of us could find information on him dating back more than two years. On the surface he looks like a great catch, but I'm afraid he may be too good to be true."

"When's the wedding?"

"I don't think they've set a date yet."

Sam's phone rang, interrupting their conversation. He spoke to a reporter in the field for a few minutes and then hung up and turned back to Dana. "The reason I called you in here was to give you a new case to work on. It concerns a friend of yours, and I thought you'd want to handle it personally."

"What friend?" Dana instantly came to attention, pushing her concerns about Casey and Tony Hunter out of her mind.

"Del Pitman."

"What's wrong with Del?" Dana's voice conveyed her concern.

"He's fine, but the new artist he's been promoting is too upset to finish the paintings he needs for the showing. It seems her husband disappeared."

"Has she called the police?"

"I don't know, but Del is beside himself. He's spent a ton of money promoting this gala event and only has three small paintings to show. She's supposed to have several more in various stages of completion, but has gone into a depression and refuses to lift a brush."

"That's strange," Dana told him. "Most artists only work on one painting at a time."

"My wife said the same thing when she told me about Del's problem." Sam's wife, Emily, worked at the Pitman Gallery on occasion. She and Dana shared an appreciation of art and both of them were artists themselves. Emily did watercolors and when Dana had moments to spare she worked on oil paintings.

"Emily is the one who actually requested my help?"

"Yes, but Del asked her to call."

"Why didn't Del call me directly?"

"He's away on business. Emily has been minding the gallery for him. When he called this morning and found out Porter hadn't delivered any of the paintings she promised him, he asked Emily to contact Globe Investigations. He wants us to find out what happened to the husband so his artist will get back to work. I went over there to have lunch with Emily and that's when she asked me if we would take the case. I wouldn't ordinarily ask you to look for a wayward husband, but since Emily asked me…" Sam shrugged.

Dana nodded. Sam ruled the newsroom and the *Globe* in general with as much strength and authority as the captain of an ocean liner, but at home, Emily steered the boat.

"Do you have the artist's name and address?"

"Right here." Sam handed Dana a sheet of paper with the Pitman Gallery's logo on it.

"Judy Porter," Dana said thoughtfully. "I met her a few months ago at one of Del's parties."

"Good. Then you don't need a special introduction to talk to the woman. Oh, and Emily said that Porter is scheduled to do some interviews next week on some of those local television talk shows and Del is afraid he'll have to cancel."

"Okay," Dana said. "I'll call her tonight and see if I can arrange a meeting for tomorrow morning."

"Since Emily is going to be at the gallery until after six, we're letting the boys fend for themselves and going out to dinner. Would you like to join us?"

"Thanks, but Bruno is off duty tonight and I promised to cook for him."

Sam grinned. "Great. You can soften him up with a good home-cooked meal and then you can ask him to check out Casey's boyfriend and get you some information on Judy Porter's missing husband."

"That's what I'm thinking," Dana replied, rising from the chair. "I was going to serve vanilla ice cream for dessert, but now I think I'll stop at the bakery on the way home and pick up an apple pie. It's Bruno's favorite."

Sam laughed. "That cop doesn't stand a chance."

TWO

WITH SOME OF THE IDEAS she and Marianne had discussed about weddings floating around in her head, Casey left the office and drove straight to the Crescent Hills Mall where she was meeting two of her girlfriends for dinner.

She wondered if she would have time to look in the bridal shop before she went to the restaurant. Her friends would be so excited when she showed them her ring. They would both be her bridesmaids for the wedding, with two of Tony's single friends as groomsmen. It was all part of the plan.

After parking her car in the lot, Casey hurried into the mall and walked toward the bridal shop. However, when she reached the shop, she didn't go inside. Instead, Casey sat down on a bench in front of the display window and stared at the lovely white gowns. The thought of her actually wearing one of those dresses and marching down the aisle to marry Tony suddenly frightened her.

What did she know about this man she had just agreed to marry? He was rich and good-looking, but his background was a mystery. She had tried to get information from him, but it had become a silly game. He answered all her questions with a question of his own.

Perhaps Tony was not being totally honest with her, but Casey was not being totally honest with him, either. Tony had been nothing but kind and loving toward her and she had convinced herself that she had a lot of nerve being suspicious of Tony when she was the one who was conning him. That's why she'd finally decided to accept the ring she wore on her left hand today. He'd already asked her several times and her girlfriends were urging her to say yes. It was, after all, a crucial part of the plan.

Casey closed her eyes and recalled the night three months earlier when the plan had been conceived.

CASEY JORDAN, Carmen Manuso and Cathy Willis had been friends since high school. They were together so much that everyone called them the three Cs.

On that fateful night, the three friends were having dinner at a new Mexican restaurant in the Crescent Hills Shopping Mall.

"I'm so tired of working," Carmen told her friends. "My boss is an ogre." Carmen worked at an insurance agency.

"Quit," Cathy said casually. "You've got great computer skills; you can find something else."

"I don't want to quit. I want to marry a rich man who will support me in the manner in which I want to become accustomed."

Casey laughed. "Don't we all."

"You can say that again," Cathy agreed.

"Except girls like us don't have the social status or contacts to meet any rich guys. All the ones I meet at the insurance agency are struggling to make ends meet like I am." Carmen shrugged her shoulders and flipped her hand through her short blond hair.

"We need to join the country club set," Cathy said. "My cousin, Lucy, works in the office there and says there are lots of eligible rich men walking around."

"Can she introduce us to some of them?" Casey asked.

"No. The help is not allowed to talk to the elite members unless they talk to her first. Well, they all know she's poor or she wouldn't be working in the office, so they act like she's invisible. That suits her fine. Lucy is happily married with two teenage boys."

"It's like one of those catch-22 things," Casey said thoughtfully. "If you're rich, you socialize with people in your own tax bracket and usually marry someone who is also wealthy. If you're middle income, like we are, you end up with a middle-income mate."

"I would love to have enough money to join that snooty country club and meet some of those rich guys." Carmen turned to Cathy, who worked at Crescent Hills Savings and Loan. "Does your bank give loans to middle-income girls who want to improve their social status?"

"If you have collateral."

"Does the country club run a background check to make sure the people that join are really well-to-do?" Casey asked her friend, the bank teller.

"I don't know."

"Can you call your cousin and find out?"

"Now?"

"Yes, right now," Casey replied.

Cathy shrugged, took out her cell phone, and dialed a number. Her cousin answered and Cathy questioned her about the membership requirements at the country club.

She hung up and repeated the information she had obtained to Carmen and Casey. "Lucy says there's an application you have to fill out, but no one checks to make sure the information is accurate. If you attach a check for the membership fee and the first year's dues, you're an instant member. The membership fee is fifteen thousand dollars and the dues are ten thousand dollars a year. Of course, that gives you unlimited access to the golf course."

Casey nodded. "So, we'd need to come up with twenty-five thousand dollars for one of us to join the club."

Carmen and Cathy both stared at Casey. Finally Carmen spoke. "What is going on in that devious mind of yours, Casey?"

Casey laughed. "Forget it. It probably wouldn't work."

"Let us be the judge of that," Cathy told her.

"Okay. We pool our money and one of us joins the country club. Once she's a member she starts socializing with the rich guys and snags herself a wealthy mate. She can also bring her two friends to the club for some of the activities and introduce them to her husband's rich friends."

"That's absolutely brilliant," Carmen exclaimed. "Let's do it."

"Wait a minute," Cathy said. "Where are we going to get twenty-five thousand dollars?"

"From your bank," Carmen answered. "We'll take out a loan and after we marry the rich guys they can pay it off for us. Only I'm not the one who is going to join the club. Casey has to do it."

"Why me?" Casey asked. "You're both more attractive than I am."

"If you'd wear some makeup and ditch the frumpy clothes, you'd be gorgeous," Cathy said. "Besides, the one who joins has to have a flexible job so she can go there during the week."

"And," Carmen added with a triumphant smile, "the one who joins should know how to play golf. Cathy and I don't know which end of the stick is which."

"They're clubs, not sticks," Casey informed her.

"My point exactly," Carmen said.

Although the girls were just kidding around at first, by the time the evening ended, they had talked it through and decided to apply for a loan, send Casey for a makeover and have her join the Crescent Hills Country Club.

"What if I don't meet anyone?" Casey asked.

Carmen answered the question. "Then next year at this time, we'll be sitting here deeper in debt than we are now, admitting that our master plan was a failure, but at least we'll have tried."

As THE MEMORY OF that fateful night faded, Casey looked up and saw Cathy approaching.

"What are you doing here, staring off into space?" Cathy said, sitting down next to Casey.

Casey was still wearing her gloves so Cathy had not spied the ring. That was good because Casey wanted to tell both of her friends at the same time.

"I was early so I sat down to wait. Let's go meet Carmen," Casey said smoothly, once again pushing the doubts she had about Tony out of her mind.

WHILE CASEY WENT OFF to have dinner with her friends, Dana carefully juggled a pie and a long loaf of French bread in one hand, while she opened the door to her apartment with the other. It was after five and on this cold February evening, it was already dark outside.

The apartment was on the second floor of a fourplex just a few miles from the downtown area and the newspaper office. Dana stepped into a living room with a round alcove of windows where her easel and painting supplies were set up ready to use at a moment's notice.

She hurried through the small dining room and past the tiny powder room into the kitchen. Dana deposited the bakery goods on the new granite countertop the landlord had installed a few weeks ago, put her keys back into her purse and carried it back to the living room.

As she walked, Dana pulled off the wool scarf that was covering her bouncy curls and removed her gloves, stuffing them into her coat pocket. She hung the scarf and her coat in the closet next to the front door. Then she carried her purse into the bedroom and prepared to change into her cooking clothes.

Her work clothes had been a pair of black slacks with a long-sleeved white and black blouse and sensible low-heeled pumps. The matching outfit was new and Dana wasn't the neatest person in the kitchen, so she quickly exchanged it for a pair of jeans, a Chicago Bears sweatshirt, socks and tennis shoes. She left on the delicate gold earrings that Bruno had given her for Christmas, but removed her watch and her blue sapphire ring and put them on her dresser.

Dana's maple bedroom set with the four-poster bed, a matching chest of drawers and a small dresser with a mirror framed in maple filled up the room. It was the same set she'd had when she lived at home with her parents on their farm in southern Illinois. Being the youngest of four children and the only girl meant that Dana always had her own room while her brothers had to share.

Her dad and her oldest brother, Paul, had moved the bedroom set from the farm when Dana's job at the newspaper began to pay enough to allow her to move from the small apartment she'd rented when she first came to Crescent Hills to work at the *Globe*. That first apartment hadn't even had a bedroom, only a sleeper sofa with springs that made a good night's sleep difficult. This bedroom had a walk-in closet and its own bathroom.

Linda and Warren Sloan still lived in the old farmhouse that had been modernized some since their children had moved out. Dana's three brothers still lived near her parents and helped them run the farm in addition to the other jobs they held in the community. Paul was a first-rate mechanic, Kevin an architect and Patrick a graphic designer. All three were married and all three had children under the age of ten that spent many happy hours at the farm with Grandma and Grandpa. Paul had three sons, Kevin had twin girls and Patrick and his wife had a boy and a girl. Like Bruno, Dana's parents and her siblings were all waiting for Dana to settle down and raise a family.

Dana went back to the kitchen and turned on the oven. Then she opened the refrigerator and removed the foil-lined pan of chicken that had been marinating in olive oil, lemon and a variety of spices since early that morning and put it in the oven to bake for an hour.

She filled the coffeemaker with water and French roast coffee and pushed the *Brew* button.

Thinking how her mom would be horrified, Dana took the box of instant mashed potatoes from a cabinet and set it next to the stove. Next she set the dining room table with her good china and put long blue candles into the candlesticks. *Nothing like a candlelight dinner to set the right mood.*

Dana returned to the kitchen and went to work on the salad. By the time the doorbell rang, it was mixed in a pretty glass bowl waiting to be adorned with dressing.

"Hi," Dana said casually as Bruno came in, slapping his gloved hands together to warm them up.

"It's freezing out there," he replied, leaning down to give her a quick kiss."

"You should wear a hat," she told him. "My mom says that when your head is cold, your whole body shivers."

"I hate hats," Bruno replied. "They make me look like a roaring twenties gangster."

"You look like one anyway," Dana said with a grin. "Come on into the kitchen and talk to me while I work on the vegetables. I've got coffee brewing."

Dana went back to the kitchen, allowing Bruno to remove

his gloves and coat and hang them in the closet. She was smiling to herself over her last comment to Bruno.

He was tall and broad with a linebacker's physique. His eyes were so dark they sometimes looked black, especially if he was angry. His hair was thick, black and curly, inviting one to lose her fingers in it.

Although his features were very attractive, like his eyes, they could become dark and menacing when he was angry. Dana always thought Bruno's looks were perfect for a cop, the kind that would scare the truth out of suspects.

Bruno came in and swung his well-toned body onto a stool at the kitchen counter. "Coffee please, miss," he said as if he were at a restaurant.

"Coming right up, sir," Dana replied, setting a mug of steaming coffee down in front of him.

"What's the special tonight?"

"Baked chicken, mashed potatoes, green beans, salad and French bread."

"And what's this?" Bruno asked, nodding toward the bakery box.

"Apple pie."

Bruno shook his head and took a sip of his coffee. "Uh-oh. Apple pie and candles on the table. You must want a big favor."

Dana dumped the frozen green beans into the vegetable steamer and turned it on. "I do not," she protested.

"Yes, you do. Ask me now and I'll think about it over dinner."

"It's not a favor," Dana said stubbornly. "I just need a little information."

"About a who or a what?"

"A who," she said, smiling sweetly. "Actually two who's."

"Go on."

"I'm not going to ask you now when you're in such a negative frame of mind."

Bruno nodded and slipped off the stool. He approached Dana with the brilliant smile that erased the darkness from his eyes and face. "Maybe I just need a hug."

"And that's all you're going to get," she replied, letting him pull her into his strong arms. "I'm cooking dinner here."

Bruno held her close for several minutes, resting his chin on the top of her curls. "Your hair smells like lemons," he said.

"I think that's the chicken," she replied. "My shampoo is supposed to make it smell like violets. Now let go of me so I can slice the bread."

Bruno laughed and released her. He returned to his stool and watched as she got out the breadboard and started slicing the long loaf of bread and placing it in a wicker basket lined with a linen napkin.

Dana poured herself a cup of coffee and drank it while she finished preparing dinner. Bruno asked about her family and she filled him in on the phone conversation she'd had with her brother Paul the night before.

"I wish I could have made the last trip with you," Bruno said a little wistfully as Dana whipped milk into the instant potato buds. "Your mom would have made me real potatoes."

"These are real potatoes," Dana said. "They're just in a more convenient form."

Bruno helped her carry the serving dishes to the table and filled the water glasses. Dana turned down the lights and lit the candles.

Since their last dispute, they had made a pact not to talk about murder and investigations during dinner. Actually they were always making that pact and breaking it, but tonight Dana made sure the conversation centered around other things.

Once the dinner dishes were cleared and Bruno had finished his second piece of pie, Dana read the look of contentment on his face and broached the subject of Casey.

"Casey is engaged," she said quickly. "Surprised us at the staff meeting today with the announcement."

"Who is she marrying?"

"A guy named Tony Hunter."

"Don't know him."

"No, and I'm afraid Casey doesn't know him, either."

"Come on, sweets. Casey is a big girl and a trained investigator. I'm sure she probably checked him out."

"She did, but couldn't come up with anything further back than two years ago when he moved to Crescent Hills."

"Is this one of the 'who's' you want me to give you a little information on?"

"Yes."

"No."

"That's not an acceptable answer."

Bruno laughed and shrugged. "That's what you always say the first time I tell you no. Then comes the arguing, then the pleading and finally a suitable bribe. Let's fast-forward to the last item."

"You've already had the last item," Dana responded. "A home-cooked dinner and two pieces of pie. That's it, buster."

"Okay, Dana, but I'm going to need more than the guy's name. Tony Hunter sounds like a name a movie studio makes up for one of their actors. Get me his fingerprints and I'll run him through the department's database and find out if he's a criminal. I assume you and Casey have already tried tracking him by his date of birth and Social Security number."

Dana nodded. "We came up with zilch, but he seems to have plenty of money. She met him at the Crescent Hills Country Club on the golf course."

"Whoa! Wait a minute here," Bruno said. "How did Casey get to play golf there?"

"Bob asked her the same thing today. She said she had an unexpected windfall and used it to join the country club."

"So Casey is rich now?"

"I don't think so. She's still working for me."

"Honey, you have to have big bucks to get into that club."

"Look, Bruno, I'm not sure how Casey got in and I don't care. I'm just worried that this Hunter guy isn't what he appears to be. He could be one of those mob guys in the Witness Protection Program, which would explain why his background begins and ends two years ago."

"Which would make it impossible for me to find out anything, either. The feds would have wiped him out of the computer database when he got his new identity."

"You went to school with that FBI guy in the Chicago office. I was thinking you could bypass the usual channels and ask him for help."

"I've seen Barry once in ten years. We're not exactly buddies anymore. I think you'd better start from the beginning and tell me why you and Casey were suspicious of this guy to begin with."

Dana sighed and sat back in her chair. "It all started about three months ago. I knew that something was up with Casey because she suddenly decided to let Marianne arrange a makeover for her. Bob got all excited and thought she was ready to get fixed up with one of his single friends, but she turned him down flat. She looks great with the new hairdo and clothes."

"Really. I haven't seen her or maybe I have and didn't recognize her."

"Anyway, a few weeks later, she told me about joining the country club, but she didn't give me any real details about how or why she did it. She really just wanted to talk about meeting Tony Hunter."

Bruno nodded and refilled his coffee cup with the insulated decanter still on the table. "So, she joined the country club, met this guy on the golf course and fell in love with him. Sounds like every young girl's dream, except for you, of course."

Dana ignored the remark and continued with her story. "Casey said that a few weeks into their relationship she started picking up little things about Tony that seemed odd. He paid for everything with cash and said he didn't believe in credit cards or checking accounts. Tony claimed to have an engineering degree and said he did freelance work for a firm in Chicago, but when Casey tried to check on the company, she learned they had been out of business for years."

"How did she get his Social Security number?"

"She went to the bank with him one day to get something out of his safety deposit box. He had to show two forms of ID to the clerk and Casey got the number while the girl was writing it down. She can read upside down, you know, and she also has a terrific memory, almost photographic."

"Okay. What else?"

"Well, once she had the Social Security number, she ran a check on him and when she discovered the information only went back two years, she began to worry. That's when we had lunch and she asked for my help, but I couldn't find out any more than she did."

"If he claims to have an engineering degree, he must have gone to college. What has he said about that?"

"Casey asked him about school, and he said he was educated by the army when he was in the service and went to school overseas."

"Clever. Harder to check."

"Then you think there is something wrong here?"

"I do. I think it's very wrong that Casey has only known this guy two months and is going to marry him, when you and I have been together for more than two years and you won't even discuss the possibility of marriage with me."

Dana stood up quickly and brought the lights up in the dining room, then blew out the candles that had already burned halfway down. She took her chair again and stared at Bruno. "Maybe the reason I don't talk about marriage with you is because when I turn to you for help and advice you give me a hard time."

Bruno reached over and grabbed her hand. "I'd never give you a hard time if you were my wife."

"That's a lie and you know it."

Bruno nodded. "It's more like a promise I'd try to keep."

"What about Tony Hunter? Are you going to help me or not?"

"I don't think you need to worry about him. Casey must have decided he's okay if she agreed to marry him."

"Maybe she just decided to ignore the problem. Women in love do that, you know."

"Okay, you win. Invite Casey and her boyfriend out for dinner this week at Marsella's. I'll arrange for my pal, Vince, to wait on us and he can nab a glass with Hunter's fingerprints."

"That's brilliant," Dana told him, breaking into a smile. "I'll ask Casey tomorrow."

"Are you happy now?"

"Yes, but I have another favor to ask."

Bruno groaned. "Okay, let's hear it."

"Who do you know in missing persons?"

"Glenn Harrison."

"If this woman I'm going to meet tomorrow has filed a report on her husband, can you get Glenn to talk to me about it? Her name is Judy Porter."

"I'll do my best," Bruno promised.

"That was too easy," Dana said suspiciously. "You didn't even ask any questions."

Bruno's cell phone rang. He looked at the caller ID and got up and went into the kitchen to answer it. That meant it was the station calling with police business.

Dana stood up and stacked up the cups and saucers and carried them into the kitchen. She could only hear Bruno's side of the conversation, but it sounded like he was being called to a crime scene. She set the dishes down on the counter over the dishwasher and waited for Bruno to finish his call.

"Have to run, honey," Bruno said when he hung up.

"What's up?"

"A corpse just floated to the surface in Crescent Lake."

"I'll walk you to the door."

Bruno and Dana walked to the front door and she watched while Bruno donned his coat. He pulled her into his arms and kissed her.

"I'll call you tomorrow. Thanks for dinner."

"Thank you for agreeing to help me with my two who's," Dana said.

"You're welcome." He kissed her once more and then opened the door and stepped into the hallway.

Dana stood in the doorway as he headed for the stairs. "Be careful out there," she said.

"I will."

Bruno went down three stairs and Dana was about to close the door when he turned around and came back. "One more thing," he said pleasantly.

"What's that?"

"My mother is coming to visit me around Valentine's Day. She'll be here at least a week, so clear your calendar."

Dana's hazel eyes widened and she tried to reach out and grab Bruno's coat, but he was already bolting down the stairs.

Bruno's mother lived in Chicago and ran the lives of her two daughters, their husbands and their children with a firm hand. She also volunteered at a local homeless shelter and played Bingo three nights a week. Dana had met her three times in the last two years and fortunately those meetings had been brief because Angelina Bruno was even more determined than her only son to change Dana from a career woman to a housewife.

THREE

JUDY PORTER'S APARTMENT was in one of the original neighborhoods in Crescent Hills. The area consisted mostly of warehouses and small businesses with buildings of wire-cut red brick.

Dana parked her car at the curb and glanced at the pizza parlor that occupied the first floor of the building. It was 9:00 a.m. and a sign in the window said the restaurant opened at 11:00 a.m. There was a wooden door next to the pizza parlor's entrance that accessed the apartments on the second and third floors of the building. When Dana had talked to Judy on the telephone the previous night, the artist told her to push the bell for apartment 2 and she would buzz her into the stairway.

As Dana pushed the bell and waited for the buzzer to sound, she noted that like her own building this one housed four apartments.

Within seconds the buzzer sounded allowing Dana to open the downstairs door so she could climb the steep stairs that lead to Porter's apartment. When she arrived on the landing, Judy Porter was standing in her open doorway waiting for Dana.

"Hi," Judy said. "The place is a total mess, but come on in."

"Thanks," Dana replied, stepping past the artist and entering the apartment.

Judy hadn't exaggerated; the place was more than a little messy.

"I made some coffee. Do you want some?" Judy asked.

Dana accepted the offer and followed Judy through a cluttered living room into the kitchen. The appliances and furnishings were old and worn and the small sink was loaded with dirty pots and pans and dishes.

Removing her coat and scarf, Dana smiled and sat down on a wobbly chair at a scarred wooden table wondering if Judy Porter would be able to find a clean cup to serve the coffee in.

Judy sighed and went to the sink. She pulled out two coffee mugs and quickly squirted dishwashing liquid into them and then rinsed them. She filled the mugs with coffee from a sleek automatic drip pot. The coffeemaker and a small microwave oven were set on the tiled counter next to the sink and looked very out of place in the old-fashioned kitchen.

"I have sugar, but the milk went bad," Judy said.

"That's okay. I drink it black," Dana replied. "Sit down and talk to me."

When Dana met the artist at the gallery a few months back, she had been impressed by her energy and vitality. She was an attractive girl with long blond hair that had been parted down the middle, worked into two neat braids and pinned to the top of her head. She had worn a floor-length black dress with slits up the sides that showed a lot of her shapely legs, but the first thing one noticed about the girl were her light blue eyes. They sparkled with humor and delight as she talked about her work and the opportunities she might find as Del's protégée. Dana had been very impressed by her and the one lovely painting that was displayed that evening.

This morning, as Judy placed the mugs on the table and sat down across from Dana, her eyes were dull and lifeless. Her hair hung straight and limp around a face that would have been completely colorless if not for the fading bruise that extended from her left eye down to her jawline. She was wearing a pair of sweatpants and a man's white dress shirt with the sleeves rolled up to her elbows.

Dana studied her for a time before speaking. Then she smiled, trying to make the girl more comfortable. "I was so sorry to hear about your husband. Have you had any word on him?"

Judy shook her head in a negative reply.

"Have you filed a missing person's report with the police?"

"Yes. I called the morning after Lucas disappeared, but the police said he had to be missing twenty-four hours before I could file a report. So I waited until the next day, hoping he'd show up on his own. When he didn't I went to the station and filed the report. I talked to a Detective Harrison. He was very nice, but when he saw the bruise on my face, he told me maybe I was better off not finding Lucas. I knew then that he wasn't going to look too hard for him."

"So Lucas hit you?"

"Not all the time," Judy said quickly. "Just once in a while when I acted crazy and he needed to calm me down."

"Did you know you were acting crazy?"

"Sure. It was mostly when I was working on a painting. Sometimes I get real uptight and emotional about my art. It's all I can think of and that makes me ignore Lucas and his needs."

"And that made Lucas angry?"

She nodded and touched her face where Lucas's fist had obviously connected with her flesh.

"Tell me what happened the last time you saw Lucas."

"I was working on one of my paintings and Lucas came

home and asked what I was cooking for dinner. I said I had to finish the painting and he could call the place downstairs and get a pizza or something. He said he didn't want a pizza; he wanted me to cook him a regular meal. I told him I didn't have anything to cook because I was working on the painting all day and didn't get to the grocery store. That's when he got mad and hit me." Judy stopped and winced as if she were seeing her husband's fist coming at her again.

"What happened then?" Dana asked kindly.

"He socked me so hard I fell down and bumped against the easel. That made my painting fall on top of me. The paint was still wet and it smeared. I started screaming at Lucas that he ruined my painting. I told him to get out and leave me alone. He picked up a tube of paint and threw it at me and then he slammed out of the apartment."

"And you haven't heard from him since?"

"No, and I'm worried sick. It's been over a week now and I can't eat or sleep I'm so upset."

"Has Lucas ever done anything like this before?"

"No. Whenever we fight and Lucas hits me, he runs out of the house, but he always comes home in a few hours. He usually brings me flowers or some other little gift. He begs me to forgive him. I do and we make up and things are good again."

"Do you know if there's a particular place Lucas goes when he leaves the house—a bar, a restaurant?"

"He usually goes to the pool hall down the block. We don't have a car right now, so he can walk there. I think it's called the Pool Palace."

"Have you checked back with Detective Harrison to see if he has any leads?"

"No. He said he'd call me if anything turned up, but I haven't heard a word. I'm so scared that something happened to Lucas that I can't function. Del expects me to deliver more paintings for the exhibit and be interviewed and stuff, but I can't paint right now. I'm too upset."

"What about Lucas's job? I assume you've checked with his employer."

"He was working at a grocery store, but he got laid off. So he signed up with one of the temporary agencies and they were sending him out on jobs. He hated most of them."

"What grocery store did he work at?"

"It was the Sunflower store on Twelfth Avenue."

Dana drew a pad from her purse and made a note. "I know the store. I shop there sometimes. Do you know the name of the temp agency?"

"I'm not sure, but his last paycheck came in the mail yesterday. It's probably on there."

"Yes, I'm sure it is. Can you get it, please?"

Judy put her hands on the table and pushed herself to her bare feet and went off to find the piece of mail. She returned with a long white envelope in her hand. It was unopened.

"You haven't opened it yet?"

"No. Lucas didn't like me opening his mail."

"Do you and Lucas have a joint checking account?"

"Yes, but he took care of all our money. I'm not good with things like that."

Dana copied down the name and address of the temp agency on her notepad and handed the envelope back to Judy. "You need to open that and deposit the check into your bank account. You also need to get a copy of the last bank statement and see what's in the account now. If Lucas left on his own, he may have taken the money from the account."

"That's what Detective Harrison said too."

"So did the detective check on it for you?"

"I don't think so. If he did, he never told me what he found."

Dana took a deep breath. She silently agreed with Detective Harrison that Judy Porter was probably better off without Lucas Porter, but the girl would need some help and guidance to stand on her own two feet again.

"Tell me, Judy. Before you and Lucas were married, did you handle your own money?"

"Not really. I lived at home and my dad took care of it. Not that there was much to take care of. I was in art school and not earning much."

"Where is your dad? Can you call on him for help?"

"He died two years ago, and my mom died when I just a baby. I really don't have any family to speak of, just Lucas and now he's—" Judy stopped as tears clouded her eyes.

Dana quickly reached across the table and grabbed hold of her hand. "Listen to me, Judy. You've got to stop feeling sorry for yourself and take some action. I'll bet you don't even know if your rent or utilities are paid, do you?"

"No," the artist whispered softly.

"I want you to take a shower and get dressed. While you're doing that, I'll clean up your kitchen for you."

"Oh, no," she protested. "I couldn't let you do that."

"I want to," Dana insisted. "I grew up on a farm where dishes were always hand-washed so I'm an expert. After you're dressed, I'm going to take you to the bank and find out where you stand financially."

"Why are you being so nice to me?" Judy asked.

"Because you are important to Del Pitman and Del is a good friend of mine. He asked me to help you and that's exactly what I'm going to do."

"Are you going to look for Lucas?"

"Yes. I'll look for Lucas, but not until I make sure you

won't get thrown out of this apartment or have your electricity turned off."

Judy's eyes widened. "Gee, I hadn't even thought of that. Lucas—"

"I know," Dana said, interrupting her. "Lucas took care of those things, but he's not here right now, so you and I will have to do it."

Judy nodded and got up from the table. Dana watched her go off in what she assumed was the direction of the bathroom.

Dana pulled up the sleeves of the brown cashmere sweater that went so well with her beige slacks and headed for the sink. As she began to stack the dishes for washing, she smiled to herself. Her mother always said that the kitchen was the center of the house and once that was in order the rest of the house and the people in it could function properly.

Dana worked quickly and had all the dishes washed and stacked neatly in the drainer by the time Judy Porter returned to the kitchen. Dana had also wiped down the table and the counter.

Judy looked around and almost smiled. "I didn't think it would matter, but having clean dishes does make me feel a little better."

"Good."

Judy's hair had been shampooed and fastened into a ponytail. She was wearing a nice blue sweater and a clean pair of jeans that hugged her hips and showed off her lithe figure. "Now what?" she asked Dana.

"Now gather up all the mail you have in the house. We need to go through it and see if there are any outstanding bills or if there is a current bank statement I can look at."

For the next half hour, Dana and Judy went through the

mail. The bank statement for the month of January was there. The names on the account were Lucas and Judith Porter. That and the fact that the difference between the beginning balance and the ending balance was the total of the checks that had been written against the account told Dana that Lucas had probably not taken any money from the checking account. There was also a savings account statement from the same bank, but the beginning and ending balance on that were the same except for a small amount of interest that had accumulated in January.

"So," Dana said. "You have a little over seven hundred dollars in your savings account and thirty-nine dollars in your checking account. All the checks written in January seem to be for January bills, rent, electric, gas and so forth. Lucas disappeared on January 29 and I doubt if he paid your rent or utilities for February."

"He told me he couldn't pay bills until his next check came from the agency." Judy picked up the still-unopened envelope and handed it to Dana. "You open it, please."

Dana quickly slit the envelope open with the edge of the kitchen knife she had been using as a letter opener. It was for $352.29. Dana glanced at the sheet of paper where she had listed Judy Porter's rent and utility amounts that totaled eight hundred and sixty dollars. "We'll have to go to the bank and deposit this check and transfer some of the money from your savings account in order to pay your February bills."

"But how can we deposit Lucas's check if he's not here to sign it?" Judy asked.

"I'll show you how," Dana said. "And since it appears that Lucas took the checkbook with him the night he left, we'll have to get money orders or counter checks from the bank to pay your bills."

Judy covered her face with her hands, seemingly overwhelmed by the tasks Dana was outlining.

Dana stood up. "Let's go, Judy. The sooner we get this banking business done, the sooner I can start looking for Lucas."

FOUR

IT WAS AFTER TWO WHEN Dana got to her office. There was a message from Del Pitman with his cell-phone number. Dana called him back to report on her morning with Judy Porter.

"First of all, Dana, let me thank you for looking into this situation for me. I owe you," Del said.

"Good," Dana replied with a smile in her voice. "Then as soon as I get some paintings done, you can host an exhibit for me."

"I'd be happy to, darling, but I'll bet you're still working on the landscape of your parents' farm."

"I'm afraid so," Dana admitted. "But I'm going to hold you to that promise. Anyway, I spent the entire morning with your artist. Did you know her husband abuses her?"

"I suspected it, but never talked to her about it."

"Judy Porter is still wearing the bruise he gave her the night he disappeared, but she wants him back. Her apartment was a mess; she was a mess. I managed to get her cleaned up and to the bank. She had Lucas's last paycheck from the temporary agency he works for and between that and some of what was in her savings account, we got her rent and utilities paid for this month."

"Was there any money missing from the account?" Del asked.

"There didn't seem to be. So that leads me to believe that Lucas probably didn't run off on his own, unless he had a rich girlfriend on the side."

"It would have to be a pretty desperate rich girl," Del told her. "Have you ever seen the lunkhead?"

"Judy gave me a photo of him and it's obvious she doesn't love him for his looks." Dana had the photo set out on her desk. Lucas Porter's body was shaped like a pear, his face was puffy, his eyes dark and beady. He was bald on top with stringy blond fringes of hair that hung down to his slumped shoulders.

"I've only met him once or twice and his personality borders on belligerence," Del said. "To be honest, if I'd met him first, I wouldn't have sponsored his wife."

"Yes, you would have," Dana insisted. "I took her to the bank and to lunch and then had her show me her studio and the paintings she's working on. She is very talented."

"She is, but if she doesn't supply me with something to sell, I've wasted a lot of time and money on her."

"Well, that's the good news, Del," Dana told him. "We had a long talk over lunch and when I left her she was back at work in her studio."

"You're a magician!" he exclaimed. "How did you manage that?"

"I told her that I would do everything I could to find Lucas, but in return she had to hold up her end of the bargain with you. I also told her that for me, painting is therapeutic, a world that I can control. She told me earlier that when she is working on her art, she loses herself in it. I hope I made her realize that sitting around crying and worrying about Lucas is not going to bring him back. She has to find comfort in her work. I also told her that February is a short month and her rent and other bills will be due again, so she had better do something to earn some money to pay them or she'd find herself and her paintings out in the street."

"If it comes to that I can help her financially," Del said.

"I know that, but Judy Porter has to learn to take care of herself."

"It sounds like you don't expect to find her husband."

"No, I don't," Dana admitted. "I only have a few leads to follow, and if those don't give me any clues to his where-abouts, I'll be stumped."

"What about Bruno? Will he help?" Del asked.

"He said he would. He's talking to the detective who works missing persons for me."

"Well, I don't care if you find the lunkhead or not. I just want my artist functioning. If she follows my directions, she can have a successful career and I can recover some of the money I've invested in it."

"I'll check on her again tomorrow and keep you posted," Dana promised.

Del thanked her again and hung up.

Dana turned her attention to the morning mail that had been opened and sorted by Marianne. There were a few new cases to assign to Bob or Casey. Thinking of Casey reminded Dana of the other problem she had asked Bruno to help her with the night before. She reached for her phone and dialed Casey's cell number.

Casey answered after four rings. "Hi, Dana," she said, reading the caller ID on her phone's message screen. "What's up?"

"Not much. I've been out of the office all morning work-ing on something Sam asked me to look into, so I missed you this morning when you checked in with Marianne."

"I just wanted to report that I took my car over to Flannery's Garage. They are supposed to do an oil change and a lube job and call me when it's ready to pick up. So far, no word from them."

"How are you getting around without a car?"

"Bob picked me up and we're working on a few other things together. Did you need to talk to him?"

"No. Actually, I wanted to invite you and Tony to have dinner with Bruno and me tomorrow night at Marsella's."

"How nice," Casey replied with no hint of suspicion in her voice. "I'll check with Tony and let you know."

"Great. Bruno's mom is coming to town this month, so I want to get together with you before she gets here."

"Have you met her before?"

"A few times. She's quite the woman; I'm a little intimidated by her. What about Tony's mom? Do you get along with her?"

"Tony doesn't have any family to speak of," Casey replied carefully. "So, I guess I don't have to worry about getting along with my in-laws."

"Well, that could be a plus," Dana told her. "Let me know about dinner."

"I will," Casey said, but her voice had lost the upbeat tone it had when they started the conversation.

Dana was sorry she had questioned Casey about Tony's family. It had reminded Casey of the doubts about her fiancé that she had come to Dana with a few weeks earlier. At that time, Casey said that Tony refused to talk about his family, claiming that they didn't get along and had no contact with one another. Now Dana wondered if he had changed his story, denying the very existence of relatives to keep Casey from asking more questions.

Dana reviewed the new cases that had come in the mail that day. Fortunately, there were only two minor problems and she assigned both of them to Bob.

Marianne just gave Dana the cases that needed a trained investigator to handle. Many requests required simple research that could be handled by a phone call or an Internet search. Marianne did most of that work herself or enlisted the help of other departments in the newspaper. Then she wrote up a report that Dana reviewed and approved before it was sent out to the client.

A few such reports were also on Dana's desk. She read the original requests from the clients and Marianne's reports on the matters, signed off on them and walked out to the reception area to return them to her secretary.

"These are good, ready to go," Dana said. "Thank you. Anything urgent in the e-mails today?"

"No," Marianne replied.

"Okay, then. I'm going to drive over to the Sunflower Market to try to talk to the manager and some of the other employees there." Dana had filled Marianne in on the case when she returned to the office after lunch. "Did you get through to the temp agency?"

"Yes. I talked to the office manager and she agreed to meet with you tomorrow morning. Here's her name and the address and phone number of the place."

Dana took the note Marianne held out to her and slipped it into the purse she already had slung over her shoulder. "If anyone is looking for me, have them call my cell phone. I probably won't be back in the office today."

With her coat and scarf over her arm, Dana left the office and headed for the elevator. When she got down to the *Globe*'s lobby, her cell phone was ringing.

Dana fished the phone out of her purse and answered it. "Dana Sloan."

"Hi, Dana." It was Casey. "The garage just called me and said that my car needs a brake job and a new water pump. The repair bill would be over three hundred dollars."

"What did you tell them?"

"I said I would have to pick the car up today and bring it back at the end of the week when I could arrange for a loaner car to drive. Bob and I are on our way back there now. Bob said it's still early enough to take it over to his friend, the honest mechanic, and have him check out the brakes and the water pump. I'll call you later."

"Thanks. I'm working on a case too, so I may not answer my cell. If it's not too late, call Marianne and give her the report. Otherwise, we'll talk in the morning."

"Sounds good," Casey replied. "Bob said this honest mechanic is one of the guys he's been wanting to fix me up with and is glad I'm going to get to meet him before I tie the knot."

The call ended with Dana and Casey both laughing at Bob's never-ending matchmaking efforts.

FIVE

SUNFLOWER MARKET was located between the newspaper building and Dana's home. The store specialized in organic produce, ethnic foods, a good variety of meat, cheeses and wines. Dana actually shopped there on a regular basis because Sunflower had a large selection of freshly prepared and packaged foods ideal for people who didn't have time to prepare their own meals.

As Dana passed by a large refrigerated case, she made a mental note to pick up a few things she could stock in her empty refrigerator and freezer.

"Hi, Miss Sloan," a man's voice called out. "Can I help you find something?"

Dana looked across the case and saw George on the other side of it, arranging packaged items in their proper order. George sometimes bagged groceries and was always eager to help the ladies carry their bags out to their cars. He was a middle-aged man with a head full of white-blond hair, faded blue eyes and a crooked smile.

"I'm looking for the manager, Ron Morgan," Dana said, walking around the case to stand next to George.

"Today's his day off. Can someone else help you?"

"Actually, maybe you can. Do you remember a guy who worked here named Lucas Porter?"

"Lucas is a creep. What do you want him for?"

"His wife asked me to try and find him. He's missing. I never saw him here, but she told me he worked here."

"You never saw him because the boss kept him working

in the storeroom. That's where everyone starts out here. If you do well in the storeroom, you get moved out into the store, where you have contact with the customers. Lucas never got to show his ugly face to the customers. He didn't last long. Got fired after a month or so."

"How long ago was that?"

"I'm not sure, maybe a month ago now."

"Was that the last time you saw him?"

"I guess." George shrugged his shoulders. "When did he go missing?"

"About a week ago. Is there anyone who works here that Lucas hung out with or knew better than others?"

"I don't think so. No one liked him, but you can ask Jose. He worked with him in the storeroom."

"Is he here now?"

"Yeah. Come on, I'll show you."

Dana followed George through the aisles that were beginning to get crowded with late-afternoon shoppers. He led her through double swinging doors into a storeroom filled with aisles of boxes and crates.

"Jose," George shouted. "Where are you?"

A short, stocky young man with black hair, a dark complexion and a nicely trimmed mustache stepped out from behind a stack of boxes. "Here. What do you want? I was taking a nap."

George laughed and introduced Jose to Dana. "She is looking for Lucas. Tell her what you know about him."

With that George turned and hurried out of the storeroom. Dana walked forward and held out her hand to Jose. He looked at her warily and ignored her outstretched hand.

"I don't know anything about Lucas. He got fired last month and I was glad to get rid of him."

"You haven't seen or heard from him since?"

"No."

"When he was working here, did he ever talk about his personal life with you?"

"Told me his wife was an artist and they were going to be rich soon."

"Anything else?"

"Yeah. He was always talking about the pool hall and how he was good at hustling the suckers there."

"That would be the Pool Palace?"

"I don't remember. He talked a lot about how great he was, but I mostly tuned him out."

"Did you ever see him outside of work?"

"Are you kidding? It was bad enough to see him here. That's it, lady. I got a lot of things to do before I can go home today and it's my little girl's birthday. I don't want to be late."

"I understand. Thank you for your help."

Dana hurried out of the storeroom and went back to George, who was still working on the case of prepared foods.

"Jose help you any?" George asked.

"Not really. I'll still need to speak to the manager."

"Sure. You want me to tell Ron to call you?"

"Yes. I'd appreciate that." Dana opened her purse and took out one of her business cards. She handed it to George and he studied it.

"Well, how about that," George said with a smile. "All the times I've seen you in here, I didn't know you were the Dana Sloan that works for the *Globe*. I read your stories all the time."

"Good. I'm glad to hear it. Just give Mr. Morgan my card and tell him I'll call him or stop by again tomorrow. I'm going to be in and out of the office most of the day."

"Sure thing," George promised. "I'll tell him." He slipped Dana's card into his shirt pocket.

"Thanks, George. I appreciate it."

Dana decided that the store was getting too crowded to do any shopping. She would just have to see if Bruno could take her to dinner tonight. Maybe he had talked to Detective Harrison and gotten some information for her on Lucas Porter.

Setting herself behind the wheel of her car, Dana glanced at her watch. She had driven over to the Pool Palace after she left Judy's apartment and found out that it didn't open for business until four on weekdays. It was still too early to go there. Her cell phone rang.

It was Bob. "Hey, boss, my friend checked out the car and said there's nothing wrong with the brakes or the water pump on the car Casey brought in to the other place. It looks like the complaints we got were valid."

"Okay. Marianne has a file on the other complaints so Casey can get more information for the article. If she can get it all put together this afternoon, we can run it in tomorrow's edition."

"Okay. Oh, and Casey said to tell you that she and Tony would love to have dinner with you and Bruno tomorrow night. She'll talk to you about the time and dress code in the morning."

"Where is she now?"

"Outside talking with Damien. He's got an old Corvette he's refurbishing and Casey wanted to look at it. Too bad she's engaged. I think Damien is interested in her."

Dana started singing the song from *Fiddler on the Roof,* "Matchmaker, matchmaker, make me a match…"

"Bye, boss. See you tomorrow," Bob said, interrupting her impromptu serenade.

Dana clicked off her phone and started the car engine.

Bob loved playing Cupid, maybe because he looked the part with his blond curly hair and chubby cheeks. No one at the newspaper had ever taken Bob's efforts seriously until Bob had fixed Marianne up with his wife's brother, Greg.

Although their first date had ended with Greg chasing a murder suspect down a dark alley, they had continued to date and Dana suspected that Marianne might be the next person in her office to announce her engagement.

Bob's success with Marianne and Greg had spread throughout the newspaper staff and now people were seeking Bob out asking if he had any good prospects for them.

Dana pushed the speed-dial button for her office and Marianne answered. She filled Marianne in on her dismal results at the grocery store.

"I still have to go the pool hall but it doesn't open until four."

"That place has a bad reputation," Marianne told her. "I hope you're not going there alone."

"I'm going to try to get Bruno to go with me, unofficially of course, but I haven't heard from him today. He got called out on a case last night, so he may be busy with that."

"Was it that gruesome one with the body they found in the lake?"

"Probably. What do you know about it?"

"Just what was on the news at noon. They said the body had been in the water for over a week and was in such bad shape, it would take time to make an identification."

A chill passed over Dana. "I didn't catch the news," she said softly. She didn't voice her fears to Marianne, but the secretary caught on anyway.

"Oh, wow. Maybe the corpse is Lucas Porter."

"Maybe. I'd better call Bruno and check on Judy Porter. If she heard that news broadcast, she could be hysterical."

Dana hung up with Marianne and dialed Judy Porter's number. The phone rang several times and was finally picked up by an answering machine.

Dana disconnected without leaving a message and dialed Bruno's cell phone number.

"Detective Bruno."

"Hi. I think the victim from your call last night may be the missing husband I'm looking for."

"Who is this?" Bruno said gruffly. "I don't answer questions from anonymous callers."

"If you don't recognize my voice by now, our relationship is in big trouble."

"Hello, Dana," Bruno said with a chuckle. "How can I help you?"

Dana sighed. "I've spent the day working with and for Judy Porter. I just tried to call her and got her answering machine. Could that be because she's at the morgue viewing the body you fished out of the lake last night?"

"Actually, she was here. She's on her way to the hospital now."

"Oh, no. It was her husband and she collapsed."

"I'm afraid so."

"Why didn't you call me?" Dana asked, not trying to hide her irritation.

"I was just going to dial your number when my cell phone rang. I'm still at the morgue. We called the paramedics for her and as they were wheeling her off, she asked me to call you. How about if I meet you at the hospital?"

"Fine," Dana said, still upset with him. "Good-bye."

SIX

CRESCENT HILLS MEMORIAL HOSPITAL was located on the other side of the downtown area. With the afternoon traffic picking up, it took Dana almost thirty minutes to get there.

She parked near the emergency room entrance and hurried inside. Bruno was at the check-in counter laughing with the pretty blonde on duty there. His laughter stopped abruptly when Dana walked up next to him.

"How is she?" Dana asked.

"I don't know. She's being checked out now. How are you?"

"Just peachy," Dana replied sarcastically. The pretty blonde had the good sense to ignore them and busy herself with some paperwork.

Bruno took Dana's arm and walked her away from the counter. "Are you jealous?" he whispered with a huge grin.

"Bruno, if I got jealous every time some girl flirted with you, or you flirted with some girl, I'd be in a straitjacket by now."

"I get jealous when you flirt," Bruno said losing the grin.

"The only guy I ever flirt with is you."

"Promise?"

"Tell me about Lucas Porter. Marianne heard a news report and she said the body was in such bad shape it would take days to identify it."

"It might have, but you know that whenever we find an unidentified corpse we check with missing persons. I did that this morning and Lucas's sheet came up along with a few others. The clincher was a tattoo on his chest that was still visible despite the time he spent in the water."

"So, you brought Judy Porter to the morgue to identify him."

"Right. She zeroed in on the wedding ring he was wearing. It matched hers and she passed out. Not that I blame the poor girl. His appearance is going to give me nightmares."

Dana let out a deep breath and sat down in the nearest chair. "Do you think it was an accidental drowning?"

"Maybe."

"Do you suspect foul play?" Dana asked urgently.

"Maybe."

"And maybe I'll speak to you again sometime this century," Dana told him, rising to her feet again.

Bruno grabbed her arm as she tried to move away from him. "Nothing has been determined yet. The autopsy is set for tomorrow afternoon."

"Bruno, you've been working homicide long enough to look at the victim and the circumstances of the case and have an educated opinion. What is it in this case?"

"Off the record?"

"Of course," she promised.

"My educated guess is that someone beat the life out of him and dumped him in the lake, probably off the Manheim Bridge where the water is too deep to freeze."

"Thank you," Dana said, allowing herself to lean into him. He put his strong arms around her and held her close while she tried to deal with the information he had just given her.

"Excuse me," a tired voice said. "I'm looking for Detective Bruno."

Bruno let go of Dana and they both turned to see a young doctor dressed in hospital greens standing behind them.

"That's me," Bruno said, walking toward the doctor.

"Mrs. Porter has been sedated and moved to a regular room. She's in shock, so we'll keep her overnight for observation. Does she have family to be notified?"

"I don't think so, but I'll check on that. I'm a friend. Can I see her?" Dana asked.

"Not tonight. I should have said, she's been heavily sedated. Are you Dana Sloan?"

"Yes."

"I'm a fan," he said with a smile. "You're much prettier than your byline photo."

Bruno grunted. Dana thanked him for the compliment.

They agreed that Dana would return in the morning to see Judy Porter and she and Bruno left the hospital.

Bruno walked Dana to her car. "I didn't get lunch today. You want to go to dinner?"

"Don't you have to report back to the station?"

"I can call in," Bruno said. "Where do you want to go?"

"I don't care," Dana said. "Sandwiches or pizza is fine with me."

"Okay. I'll follow you back to your place so you can leave your car. We can go to that café you like around the corner from you."

"Fine."

Dana unlocked her car and started to slide into the driver's seat. "Hey," Bruno said. "You're really upset about this, aren't you?"

Dana nodded. "I don't even know the guy and what's

more, from what I found out about him today, I don't even like him. But I'm really worried about Judy Porter. The girl is going to be totally on her own now and I don't know if she can handle it."

"Well," Bruno said softly, "she won't be totally alone, will she? If I know you, and I think I do, you're going to be right by her side, helping her stabilize her life."

Dana nodded again. "I'm going to try to do that."

"That's fine," Bruno said. "Just promise me you'll leave the investigation into her husband's death up to me."

"I'll see you at my place," Dana said, sliding into the car and pulling the car door closed.

Bruno stood outside shaking his head at her through the car window. "Here we go again," he said to himself as Dana started her car and drove away.

SEVEN

By the next morning, the news that Lucas Porter was a homicide victim was reported in the *Globe* and announced in the morning radio and television news broadcasts.

When Bruno called the station to report in, he was told that the coroner's preliminary findings confirmed that Lucas was a victim of foul play. He was also told that the reporters who hung around the station and the morgue hoping to pick up newsworthy items were already working on their stories. This meant that Dana didn't have to keep the assessment that Bruno had given her at the hospital off the record any longer. It also meant Bruno couldn't blame her for leaking the story.

Dana called the temporary agency and spoke to the office manager, a woman named Catherine Jankowich. She told her she would stop by before noon to talk to her. Dana also called Ron Morgan at the Sunflower Market and told him she would be by after noon to talk to him.

"The police have already been here," Morgan said. "I told them everything I know about the guy."

"That's good, but I'd still like to speak to you," Dana told him.

"George tells me you're a customer here, so I'll be glad to talk to you anytime," he said cordially.

The weather was still bitterly cold, so Dana dressed in layers. She wore a light blue sweater under a navy blue pantsuit and her ankle-high boots with the plush lining. Since her apartment building didn't provide covered parking, she left early to warm up her car and scrape off the frosty coating of ice that had settled on her windshield overnight.

Dana arrived at the hospital, found out what room Judy Porter was in, and went to see her. The artist was sitting up in bed, staring into space. Her face was as white as the hospital gown she wore.

Judy didn't notice Dana's presence in the room until she spoke to her. "Hi, Judy. How are you doing today?"

The girl turned and looked at Dana, she shook her head but didn't speak.

"I'm so sorry about Lucas," Dana said softly.

Judy nodded.

"Is there anyone I can call for you? Did Lucas have any family that should be notified?"

"I was his only family," she whispered. "And he was my only family."

"What about friends?"

"I don't know. My head feels like it's filled with water. I can't think."

"I understand. Has the doctor been in to see you this morning?"

"Yes. He said I had to go home. Are you here to take me home?"

"Yes. I'd be glad to take you home. Is there someone I can call to stay with you today?"

"My neighbor, Sally, called me early when she heard the news on the radio. She said she'd help me out."

"Good. I called Del last night and he said he'd be home tomorrow and he'd come to see you."

"Del?"

"Del Pitman, from the gallery," Dana explained.

"Oh, God," Judy said as her eyes filled with tears. "Del will want me to finish the paintings, won't he?"

"Not right away," Dana told her. "When I told him about Lucas, Del said he would postpone your showing."

Judy nodded and swiped at her tears with the sleeve of her hospital gown. "He's going to lose lots of money, isn't he?"

"He'll lose some," Dana agreed.

"I can't believe this is happening," she said. "The police told me last night that Lucas had an accident, but this morning Sally told me the news report said he was murdered. They're going to think I killed him."

"No, Judy. I don't think the police will suspect you." Even as she said it, Dana realized that the police might very well suspect Judy Porter. It was standard procedure when someone died to look closely at the person's spouse. And given the fact that Lucas Porter had abused the girl probably for years, Judy had a motive.

"You can't let them arrest me," Judy said. "I didn't do it. Please promise me you'll find out who really killed Lucas, so I don't go to jail."

Judy's tears were flowing freely now and Dana was afraid that the girl was going to get hysterical or go into shock again. "Listen to me, Judy," Dana said sternly. "You've got to pull yourself together. I can't help you unless you start thinking and acting rationally."

The artist looked at Dana and stopped crying. "There were lots of times when I thought about killing Lucas," she said. "But I didn't do it. I swear I didn't. You've got to believe me."

"I believe you, Judy."

"And you'll help me?"

"Yes. I promise."

AN HOUR OR SO LATER, Dana drove Judy back to her apartment. Her neighbor, Sally Larson, a middle-aged woman who lived down the hall from Judy, came over a few minutes after they arrived. She introduced herself to Dana and took charge of Judy. She seemed to have a motherly interest in the artist, so Dana felt confident that Judy was in good hands.

Dana was about to leave when there was a knock on the door.

"That's probably Teddy," Sally said, brushing past Dana to open the door. "He's been worried sick about Judy."

Teddy turned out to be a very blond, very nice-looking young man in his early twenties. He was dressed in khaki pants and a shirt with Brown's Hardware embroidered across the left pocket. He went straight to Judy and took her hands in his.

"I'm so sorry about Lucas. Are you okay?"

"No," Judy said as tears misted her light blue eyes again.

"I can't stay long. I'm on my lunch break, but I wanted to see you and see if there was anything I could do for you."

Judy nodded and Dana noted how she grasped Teddy's hands tighter.

Sally Larson finally realized that Dana was watching the tender scene with interest. "Teddy, I want you to meet Dana Sloan. She's the newspaper reporter who has been helping Judy. She was kind enough to bring her home from the hospital."

Reluctantly, Teddy let go of Judy's hands and turned toward Dana. "I'm pleased to meet you, Miss Sloan."

"Do you live in the building too?" Dana asked.

"Teddy is my son. He lives with me," Sally said hastily.

"Well, it seems that Judy is in good hands, so I'll be

going. I'll check back with you later, Judy," Dana said as she left the apartment.

Dana puzzled over Judy's relationship with her neighbor's son as she drove over to the temp agency where Lucas Porter had been employed. Teddy seemed to be somewhat younger than Judy, yet he was definitely smitten with the artist.

The temp agency was located in a storefront, one of several that lined the street where small retail outlets had once offered various products to the public. With the growth of Crescent Hills came shopping malls with shops that were part of large chains that forced the smaller businesses to close their doors.

It was a few minutes before eleven and Catherine Jankowich was waiting for Dana in her empty office.

"All of the jobs have been filled for today, so people don't hang around here after that," Catherine told her. She was a big woman with gray hair and large blue-rimmed glasses. "I transferred the phones to the service. Have a seat."

"Thank you."

Dana sat down in a straight-backed wooden chair in front of Jankowich's metal desk. Stacks of files and a computer filled up the desk. The woman took a file folder off the top of a stack and handed it to Dana.

"I heard about Lucas on the radio when I was driving to work this morning. That's a list of the jobs he worked for me."

Dana opened the folder and glanced at the two names on the list, CH Metal Works and Tip Top Cleaners. "What did he do at these places?"

"He worked behind the scenes in both places. Lucas wasn't the type owners would want to interact with their customers. He cleaned up at the metal works, sweeping, mopping, that type of thing. It was a short assignment while their regular man was out sick for two days."

"What about the cleaners?"

"Lucas had been working there for two weeks and was supposed to be hired permanently. Again, he worked in the back sorting the clothes for either laundry or dry cleaning. Of course, when he didn't show up on the third week, they called and I sent someone else out there."

"Did you receive any complaints about Lucas?"

"No."

"Any word of problems he may have had with other employees at either place?"

"No. I thought he was a little creepy, but he seemed to be dependable and a hard worker and that's mainly what I need here."

The door behind Dana opened and she turned around to see Bruno standing there. "Hi," Dana said, ignoring the scowl on his handsome face.

"I thought that was your car out there," Bruno said shortly.

Catherine Jankowich stood up and walked around her desk to greet Bruno. She held out a hand and smiled broadly. "Catherine Jankowich," she said sweetly. "How can I help you?"

"Detective Al Bruno, Crescent Hills Police," Bruno replied, showing her his shield. "I'm investigating the death of Lucas Porter. I understand he worked for you."

"Yes. Miss Sloan and I were just discussing that."

"Why is that?" Bruno asked her.

Catherine stepped back and looked at Dana. "Because she asked me to give her some information. Is there a problem?"

Dana stood up. "No problem. Thank you very much, Mrs. Jankowich."

"It's Miss Jankowich," the woman said, turning her gaze back to Bruno.

Dana handed her the folder and walked around Bruno and out the front door. She thought maybe he would follow her outside to give her a hard time, but he didn't. Dana hurried to her car and drove off to talk to the owners of CH Metal Works and Tip Top Cleaners.

The owners of both places were pleasant and accommodating, but neither had any information on Lucas Porter that was worth the time and gasoline Dana expended in order to interview them.

Her last stop was Sunflower Market. The manager had told her that morning that he had already spoken to the police, so Dana hoped Bruno wouldn't show up while she was talking to the man.

George was at the front this morning, bagging groceries at one of the checkout counters. He smiled and waved at Dana as she made her way past him to Ron Morgan's office. Morgan was a tall, nicely built black man in his early fifties.

"Thank you for seeing me," Dana said, shaking his hand. "I know you must be busy."

"We will be shortly. Lots of folks come to our deli counter for lunch."

"I know. When I'm in the area I stop here myself."

The office was small and cramped with a desk that was cluttered with papers and boxes and two chairs. They sat down and Dana asked him what he could tell her about Lucas Porter.

"He was an okay worker, but he didn't get along with Jose, who has been here for years. Jose was threatening to quit, and I didn't want to lose him, so I fired Porter."

"Oh, I see," Dana said. This was the most interesting

information she had gotten so far. "How did Lucas take the dismissal?"

"He didn't seem to care much. Told me his wife was about to make a bundle with her paintings and he didn't need my crummy job."

"Besides Jose, did Lucas have problems with any of the other employees?"

"No one liked him, but I wouldn't say there were problems. At least none that would lead to physical violence."

"What about Jose?"

"He's the last person who would resort to violence. Jose is a very religious man and the fact that he couldn't get along with Lucas really bothered him. That's why he wanted to quit. He was actually pretty upset when I let Lucas go. He even came in here and asked me to take the guy back as he didn't want to be responsible for having a man lose his job."

"What did you tell him?"

"I told Jose what Lucas said, that his wife was going to be so successful he didn't need to work here. Jose accepted that because Lucas was always telling him the same thing."

Dana thanked Morgan for his time and left the store. She walked across the parking lot toward her car. As she walked she took her cell phone from her purse and saw that she had three missed calls, all of them from Bruno.

It was freezing outside and Dana picked up her pace, wanting to get inside her car and out of the winter wind. She would start the engine and turn the heater on before she returned Bruno's calls. However, before she got to the car she saw Bruno's unmarked police vehicle pull up and park next to her blue Mustang. He had parked on the passenger side of Dana's car, so she ran around to the driver's side and got inside the car before Bruno could get out of his car and stop her.

Dana unlocked the passenger door and Bruno struggled inside the Mustang, which was too small for a man his size.

"I've been calling you," Bruno told her.

"I know. I was going to call you back, but it seems it's not necessary now. What do you want?"

"I want to tell you to butt out of my investigation."

Dana stared back at him defiantly. "I'm not jeopardizing your investigation. I'm trying to help a friend, two friends actually."

"That's how the trouble always starts," Bruno replied. "You've been two steps ahead of me all morning."

"I'm sorry. I guess I should have let you go first."

"My mother is coming to visit. I don't want to be fighting with you while she's here."

"Fine, we can put our argument on hold and resume it after she leaves," Dana suggested.

Bruno sighed. "I talked to the store manager early this morning at his home. I got nothing. What did you get?"

"Nothing," Dana admitted. "What did you get from the office manager? She looked like she'd try hard to impress you."

"She did, but she had nothing useful to tell me. Then I went to the metal works place and just missed you there, and it was the same story at the cleaners. The morning has been a big fat zero."

"Same here," Dana told him. "It doesn't seem that Lucas Porter was liked by anyone, but there doesn't seem to be anyone who hated him enough to kill him."

"What about his wife? Harrison told me he beat her up on a regular basis."

"Impossible," Dana declared. "She couldn't have knocked him out and threw him off a bridge."

"Maybe she had help."

"Who?"

"That's what I'm going to find out."

"You're way off base, Bruno."

"How about some lunch?" he asked, ignoring her remark.

"We're having dinner tonight at Marsella's with Casey and her fiancé. I told you last night. Did you set it up with your friend Vince?"

"Vince and I have a standing arrangement. I give him the signal and he does what I need. And just because we're having dinner together doesn't mean we can't have lunch as well. How about it?"

"Okay, on one condition. If you're going to question Judy Porter today, you have to let me come with you. The girl is a wreck and she needs my support."

"Okay, on one condition. You are to be a silent by-stander."

"Agreed. And after you question her, we can go to the pool hall where Lucas hung out. It's right by her house and opens early today."

"What pool hall?"

Dana smiled at him. "Well, it seems I did uncover some-thing useful after all, and I'm sharing the information with you, like I always do."

Bruno shook his head and reached for the door handle. "I'll meet you at Big Lou's."

Dana watched as Bruno maneuvered himself out of her car and went back to his own vehicle. She was sure that their argument over her involvement in his case would continue over lunch, but she hoped that Big Lou's home-style cooking would soften him up a bit.

EIGHT

DANA AND BRUNO ARRIVED at Judy Porter's door at 2:00 p.m. Sally answered the door and told them that Judy was in her studio working. Dana was surprised, but didn't say anything.

Bruno asked Sally to go get the artist. The living room of the apartment was a lot neater than it had been when Dana brought Judy home that morning. She assumed that Sally had been straightening it up for Judy.

Judy Porter came into the room dressed in the same clothes she had worn home from the hospital, but she had combed and braided her long hair and put on makeup.

Bruno showed her his badge and reminded her that they had met the night before. Then, he explained that Dana was there as a friend and could not help Judy answer any of his questions. The artist nodded and sat down on the sofa. Dana walked over and sat down next to her.

"I'll leave, so you can have some privacy," Sally said quickly.

"I'll want to talk to you after I interview Mrs. Porter," Bruno told her. "What is your apartment number?"

"I'm right across the hall," Sally said, looking apprehensive.

Bruno wrote down Sally Larson's name and opened the door for her. She hurried out of the apartment and Bruno turned his attention to Judy and Dana, who were silently waiting for him.

"How are you feeling, Mrs. Porter?" Bruno asked in a solicitous tone.

"I'm okay," the artist replied.

"I understand that you've been working on your paintings since you came home from the hospital this morning. I'm a little surprised that you felt up to working given the tragedy of your husband's death."

"I could have just sat here with Sally and screamed and cried, or I could have taken the sedatives the doctor at the hospital gave me and knocked myself out, but some of the things Dana told me yesterday and again this morning made me go into my studio instead."

Bruno looked at Dana and she shrugged and smiled.

"I see. And exactly what did Dana tell you?"

"She reminded me of how much Del Pitman was counting on me to produce some paintings he could sell. She also told me that my artwork took me into a world I could control, that it would help me deal with my problems. When we went to the bank yesterday she had to show me how to write checks and deposit money into my account. She said that if Lucas didn't return I would have to stand on my own and take care of my finances. That's the other reason I'm working on my paintings. They're going to be my only source of income."

Bruno nodded. "Does that mean Lucas didn't have any life insurance?"

"Oh, I didn't think of that. Yes, I think there is a policy. Do you want me to get it?"

"Yes, please," Bruno said kindly.

Judy got up and left the room. She came back a few minutes later with an insurance policy folded neatly into a plastic sleeve.

"It was in the dresser," she said simply as she handed it to Bruno.

Bruno took out the policy, unfolded it and looked at it closely. He made a note on his pad and handed the policy back to the artist without comment.

Dana couldn't keep herself from reading the declarations page over Judy's shoulder. The amount of insurance was $250,000.

Judy gasped and her hand flew to her mouth. The policy fell to the floor. Dana bent over and picked it up to look through it more closely. She noted that the premium was due quarterly and she remembered seeing a canceled check written to the insurance company the month before.

"A quarter of a million dollars should help you stabilize your finances," Bruno remarked in an emotionless voice.

"Lucas took care of all this stuff. There's a policy in his drawer with my name on it too. Do you want to see that one?"

"No," Bruno told her. "I have the report that Detective Harrison wrote up when you reported Lucas missing. It says he left the apartment that night, but it doesn't mention what you did after he left."

"I put ice on my face and sat here waiting for Lucas to come home."

"Can anyone verify that?"

"What do you mean?" Judy asked.

"I mean did your neighbor, Sally, see you here? Did anyone call you on the telephone? Did you order a pizza or any other food that was delivered to your door?"

"You think I killed Lucas?" Judy yelled.

Dana grabbed her arm to keep her from standing up to confront Bruno. "Judy, calm down," she said urgently. "These are just routine questions."

Bruno glared at Dana, warning her to keep the silence she had promised him.

Judy sat back and took a deep breath. "I didn't kill my husband," she told Bruno.

Bruno ignored her statement and asked another questions. "Were you and your husband faithful to each other?"

"I want a lawyer," Judy Porter said. She turned to Dana. "Can you get me one?" she asked. The girl's fear and panic showed in her eyes.

"I can," Dana replied.

The artist turned back to Bruno. "This interview is over, Mr. Bruno. I refuse to answer any more questions without my lawyer present."

Bruno was surprised at the abrupt change in her manner, but he sighed, closed his notebook and stood up. "Very well. Tell your lawyer to call me and we'll make arrangements to continue this interview at the police station tomorrow morning at 10:00 a.m."

"They'll be there," Dana said, answering for the artist who had now slumped back onto the sofa like a rag doll.

Dana got up and walked Bruno to the door and ushered him into the hallway. "I still want to go to the pool hall with you," she whispered.

"Of course you do," Bruno whispered back. "I suppose you want to go with me to question the neighbor too?"

"Yes, but I'm going to stay here with Judy and get her calmed down. You question the neighbor and come back for me when you're done."

"I love it when you tell me how to conduct an investigation. I'll pick you up at seven for dinner."

Dana grabbed his arm but he walked away and she had no choice but to be dragged along with him. He stopped at Sally Larson's door. "Fine," Dana said. "I'll get Judy settled and go to the pool hall myself."

CAROL COSTA

"No, you won't," Bruno warned. "That's not a place for a woman to enter on her own."

"Either you take me in there or I'm going in by myself," she said stubbornly.

"Then you can forget about me helping you run a trace on Casey's boyfriend."

"Are you blackmailing me?" Dana asked.

"I'm trying to keep you safe and out of my homicide case."

If it weren't for Casey, Dana would have told Bruno to take a long walk off a short pier. However, she had just thought of another way she could check out the pool hall.

"I'm sorry," Dana said with as much sincerity as she could muster. "You're right. I'll be ready at seven and we can talk about some nice things to do with your mother when she visits. Maybe Casey or Tony will have some ideas."

Bruno's look softened, but still conveyed distrust. "No tricks? You promise you won't step foot in that pool hall?"

"I promise."

Bruno bent down and kissed her lightly. "I'll see you at seven. Get a good lawyer for the artist."

He knocked on the door he was standing in front of, and Dana hurried back to Judy Porter's apartment.

Judy was still on the sofa in the same position. Dana went directly to the phone and called Sam McGowan. "I need a good criminal attorney," she said when Sam answered.

"For you?"

"No. Judy Porter."

"Is she Bruno's number one suspect?"

"Yes. I'm at Judy's apartment now," Dana told him

pointedly. "Have the attorney call me here and I'll give him the details."

"Will she be able to pay a fee?"

"Yes."

"Okay. I'll see what I can do. Either I'll call you back or the lawyer will. What's the number there?"

Dana gave Sam the number. "You can also call my cell phone," she added.

Dana hung up and went over and sat down next to Judy. "It's going to be okay, Judy," she said firmly. "My editor knows some of the best attorneys in town. He'll get you someone really good."

"I told you the police would want to arrest me," Judy replied. "They always suspect the wife."

"The amount of that insurance policy didn't help matters," Dana told her.

"I can't believe it's so much. Lucas never told me."

"I believe you," Dana said. "Why don't I make us some coffee while we wait?"

Judy nodded in agreement as she carefully refolded the insurance policy and slipped it back into its plastic sleeve. Dana went off to the kitchen to make coffee and use her cell phone to call her office.

"Hi, Marianne," she said when the secretary answered. "Is Bob there?"

Bob was in the office writing up a report on one of the cases he had investigated. Marianne connected him with Dana.

"Bob, I need your help. There's a seedy pool hall I need to check out and Bruno has forbidden me to go in the place. It's three o'clock now. Can you meet me there at four-thirty?"

"You're going to send me in there instead?"

"Right."

"Sounds like fun. I'll be there."

"Good. Here's the address."

Dana gave Bob the address and then clicked off her phone. Bruno would question Sally Larson and then go to the pool hall to ask questions. He should be on his way back to the station by four at the latest.

NINE

MARSELLA'S WAS A delightful Italian restaurant with intimate tables and excellent food. Bruno's mother knew the owners, so Bruno was always treated royally when he came in for dinner.

It was a little after seven when Bruno escorted Dana through the door and they were greeted warmly by the hostess, who took their coats and gave them to another girl to hang up in the cloak room.

"There'll be four of us tonight," Bruno told her. "And we want to be seated in Vince's section."

"He'd throw a fit if I sat you anywhere else," the woman replied.

They slid into a private booth toward the back and Vince hurried over to say hello and see if they wanted anything to drink. Bruno told him they would wait until the other couple arrived.

"Very good. And don't worry, I will take care of everything," Vince said with a knowing nod at Bruno. "And, Miss Dana, you look very beautiful tonight."

"Thank you," Dana replied.

Vince went off to check on one of his other tables.

"You know, we'll probably have to come back here again when my mom visits," Bruno said.

"Of course," Dana said sweetly.

"So, did you get a lawyer for Mrs. Porter?" Bruno asked. It was the first time since he picked Dana up at her apartment that there had been any mention of the Porter case.

"Troy Kimball."

"Don't know him."

"He's new in town, but came highly recommended. You'll meet him tomorrow."

Bruno nodded and reached for Dana's hand. "Look, sweets, I'm sorry if I bullied you this afternoon. I know you're just trying to help the artist."

"I've already forgotten it," Dana assured him.

"This is a surprise. I thought you'd want to know what I found out at the pool hall."

"Would you tell me?"

"No."

"Then I won't ask," Dana said. "Oh, there's Casey now."

The hostess led Casey and Tony Hunter to the table. Bruno stood up and shook hands with Hunter as Casey introduced him. Hunter reached across the table and took Dana's hand as well.

"Hi, Dana," Tony said in a rich baritone voice. "I've heard a lot of wonderful things about you."

"I'm happy to meet you," Dana replied, withdrawing her hand from his grasp.

Casey slid into the booth and Tony slid in next to her. He was average looking with close-cropped brown hair and brown eyes. He was just a little taller than Casey, and like her, had a slim, athletic build. Looking at the two of them sitting across the table Dana couldn't help thinking they could pass for brother and sister rather than boyfriend and girlfriend.

"You two match," Bruno said, referring to the fact they both wore olive green sweaters with white collars.

Casey laughed. "We went to the mall last night and couldn't resist that new his-and-her shop. We got these sweaters in green and blue."

A busboy came over and filled their water glasses. Vince

appeared right behind him and everyone agreed to share a bottle of red wine.

They sipped wine and ordered dinner, chatting about nonessentials like the cold weather and the odds that the Chicago Bears would make the playoffs that year.

"I'm not a football fan," Tony admitted. "Basketball is my game of choice."

"Dana and I are Bulls fans," Bruno said. "But since the dream team broke up, we haven't had a lot to cheer about."

"I prefer college ball," Tony told him.

During dinner Casey and Tony talked about how they had met on the golf course at the country club right before Thanksgiving. "It was too cold for most golfers to be out on the greens. The grass was already turning brown, but it wasn't frozen yet, so I thought it would be a good time to practice," Casey said. "Tony thought the same thing, and we ended up playing eighteen holes together."

"And that was the start of a beautiful friendship," Tony added.

Vince came over and picked up Tony's wineglass. "Oh, I forgot something," he said. "I'll be right back." He hurried off with only Tony's glass, holding it carefully by the stem.

The waiter returned in a few moments with a cart containing coffee and a dish of assorted Italian pastries.

"Those look scrumptious," Dana said.

"Compliments of the house for my favorite customers," Vince said cheerfully. "Enjoy!" He poured coffee for everyone and then deftly gathered the rest of the wineglasses, placed them on his cart and went away.

Tony didn't seem to notice the special treatment his wineglass had received and the conversation turned to wedding plans.

"Tony wants to get married in Las Vegas," Casey said.

"It's a lot warmer there," Tony added.

"I thought you'd want a church wedding," Dana said, directing her comment to Casey. "Won't your mother be disappointed?"

"No. My cousin, Lisa, got married there at the Excalibur Hotel and it was fabulous. That's where we're thinking of going."

"It sounds good to me," Bruno said. "I'd love to escape the cold for a few days. I will be invited, won't I?"

Everyone laughed. "It's going to be a small wedding, just family and close friends, but you and Dana are definitely invited," Casey assured them.

Dana had to admit that on the surface Tony Hunter seemed like a perfectly nice guy and a good match for Casey. She tried asking him a few routine questions about where he was from and how he ended up in Crescent Hills. He was very smooth and succeeded in changing the subject without appearing rude.

Tony offered to pay the check when it came, but Bruno insisted that it was his treat. Bruno took out his wallet to extract a credit card. His badge was attached to the front of it. Tony stared at it.

"You're a cop?" Tony asked.

"Homicide detective," Bruno answered. "That's how I met these two lovely women sleuths."

"I thought I told you," Casey said.

Tony laughed. "You probably did, darling," he said, putting his arm around her. "But I'm often distracted by your beauty."

Casey blushed. Dana smiled. Bruno grunted.

They stopped at the cloakroom to get bundled into their coats. Casey, Tony and Dana walked out the door but the owner of the restaurant came out of the kitchen and engaged Bruno in a conversation so he stayed behind.

"I meant to ask you, Dana," Casey asked while they were standing outside waiting for Bruno. "Did Bob find out anything useful for you at that sleazy pool hall this afternoon?"

"What pool hall?" Bruno's voice boomed from behind them and the girls jumped at the sound of it. It seemed that Bruno's conversation with the owner had ended quickly.

"We'll talk about it on the way home," Dana told him quickly. Then she turned to Tony and held out her hand. "It's been a pleasure, Tony. I hope to see you again before the wedding."

Tony took her hand and then he and Casey said their good-byes to Bruno and thanked him again for dinner. Casey and Dana hugged long enough for Casey to whisper an apology for asking about the pool hall.

Bruno's car was directly in front of the restaurant while Tony's was around the side in the parking lot. The two couples went their respective ways. Bruno's face was dark and grim as he opened the door to his car and helped Dana inside.

The truce that Bruno and Dana had been honoring had come to an abrupt end. He started the engine of the big black SUV he drove for pleasure and pulled away from the curb. Dana sat silently, waiting for him to voice his anger.

Bruno waited until he had to stop for a traffic signal before he turned to her. "You broke your promise," he said.

"No, I didn't," Dana replied. "I promised not to go into the pool hall and I didn't go into the pool hall. I called Bob and had him do it for me."

"It's the same thing, Dana. Bob works for you."

"It's not the same thing," she insisted. "And no matter how angry it makes you, I can't stay out of this case. It was assigned to me by my editor and I have to see it through."

The light changed and Bruno stepped on the gas gently, instead of stomping on it like he usually did, strangely enough, Bruno drove more slowly and carefully when he was angry about something.

"It wasn't a murder investigation then."

"I can't help that it turned into one," she said defensively. "You always act like I can just abandon the people I'm trying to help when the police get involved in one of my cases. And you have to admit that my investigators and I have provided valuable information to the police on a number of cases."

"And that scares the hell out of me," Bruno said. "You were almost killed because of the last case you got involved in."

"I don't need to be reminded," Dana told him. She remembered all too well being trapped in an alley with a crazed serial killer. She had been wearing long-sleeved sweaters and shirts ever since to cover the scar across her upper arm that was fading slowly.

Bruno pulled into the parking lot next to Dana's building and shut off the engine. He got out of the car and came around to open the door for her.

"I don't think you should come up for coffee tonight," Dana said.

"No, you're right, but I'm coming up anyway."

Bruno took her arm and walked her to the front hallway of the building and up the stairs to her apartment. She opened the door and walked into the living room, taking off her coat and scarf and throwing them across the back of the sofa. Bruno did the same.

"So, do you want some coffee?" Dana asked.

"Yes."

The two of them went into the dark kitchen. Dana switched on the light and headed for the coffeepot. Bruno settled himself on one of the stools at the counter. They waited silently while the coffee brewed, both of them giving the other a chance to calm down.

When the coffee mugs were filled, Dana sat down next to him at the counter and waited for him to speak first.

"What did Bob find out at the pool hall?" Bruno asked.

"What did you find out at the pool hall?" Dana asked, directing his question back at him.

"I'm going to tell you what I found out," Bruno said. "Because I know you probably found out the same thing, and it should have convinced you that Judy Porter is not the innocent, naive girl you thought she was."

Dana took a deep breath and sipped her coffee. Apparently Bruno did get the same information from Lucas Porter's friends at the pool hall. Lucas complained to everyone that Judy wanted to dump him because she was having an affair with Teddy Larson who lived across the hall from them. Lucas also said he had supported Judy for years and that now that she was going to be a rich and famous artist, he wasn't going to let her dump him for another guy. He was going to stick to Judy like glue.

"Bob said most of the guys in there wouldn't make reliable witnesses," Dana finally said. "And besides, it's just hearsay."

"I've already talked to the boyfriend, who also yelled for a lawyer. The two suspects and their lawyer are all coming in first thing in the morning."

"I still think Judy is innocent," Dana said stubbornly.

"She may not have done the actual deed, but she's an accessory."

Dana stood up. "Go home, Bruno. I'm too tired to continue this argument tonight."

Bruno stood up and put his arms around her. "Sorry, babe. You can't be right all the time."

"Did you get the wineglass?" Dana asked, suddenly remembering Casey and Tony Hunter.

"One of my officers stopped there and picked it up from the kitchen before we even left the restaurant."

"Good. Thank you," Dana said, still resting her head against his broad chest. "I'll walk you to the door."

"So, I don't even get a second cup of coffee?" he asked, resting his head against the top of her head.

"I'm not dropping the Judy Porter case," Dana said.

Bruno sighed and released her. He left the apartment a few minutes later without even kissing her good-bye.

TEN

It snowed during the night and driving to the office the next morning was an exercise in patience. The streets were icy and the motorists were ill-tempered.

"Sam's in your office," Marianne told her as soon as she came through the door.

"Hold my calls," she replied.

Sam was sitting in Dana's chair, looking out the window at the icicles that were suspended from the overhang of the building across the street. He exchanged greetings with Dana as she came in and hung up her coat and scarf on the coat tree in the corner of her office.

"Have you talked to Bruno this morning?" Sam asked, relinquishing Dana's chair to her and walking around the other side of the desk.

"No. I doubt if he would take my call."

"Sorry. What's new on the Porter case? Emily expects me to call her with a full report this morning."

"Is she still working at the gallery?"

"No. Del came back last night. He heard about Lucas being murdered and called Emily. I guess he tried to call you but couldn't get through."

"After Bruno left, I turned off my cell and unplugged my landline."

"Uh-oh. This sounds serious."

Dana nodded and proceeded to tell Sam what Bob found out at the pool hall the previous afternoon. "Of course, Bruno got the same story and immediately went after

Teddy and ordered him to show up for questioning at the station this morning with Judy."

"So Bruno thinks that Judy and her boyfriend killed her husband. What do you think?"

"I don't know. They claim to be just friends. I talked to both of them after Bruno was done with them yesterday. Teddy looks like a choirboy. I'm having a hard time seeing him as a murderer. By the way, I arranged for Troy Kimball to represent Teddy as well as Judy this morning. Another thing Bruno will get steamed over when he finds out."

"I'd say you've done all you can, Dana. Let the police and the lawyers handle it now."

"I may have to do that, but first I'm going to the gallery to talk to Del."

What Dana didn't tell Sam was that Del Pitman was the most inquisitive person she had ever met and that he just might have some inside information to share on Judy, Teddy and Lucas.

Sam left and Marianne came in with some messages. One of them was from Floyd Flannery of Flannery's Garage.

"I assume this one is about the story Casey wrote blowing the whistle on his unethical business practices," Dana said holding the message up for Marianne to see.

"You don't have to call him back. He just called to say he was going to sue the *Globe* for printing a bunch of lies."

"I assume Casey made a file with all her backup information in it."

"She always does, but she didn't leave it with me."

"Can you call her and remind her to bring it in?" Dana asked. "If Flannery gets a lawyer, Sam will want the file immediately."

"I already tried to call her this morning, on her cell phone and her land line. No answer either place."

"That's strange. She didn't say anything about needing the day off. Bruno and I had dinner with her and Tony last night."

"You did? What is he like?" Marianne sat down in the one of the brocaded chairs in front of Dana's desk. It was obvious that Marianne wasn't going to move until she got some details from Dana.

"He looks like a perfect match for Casey—tall, slim, attractive. They were even wearing matching sweaters. We had a nice time. They're thinking of getting married in Las Vegas."

"That would be fun," Marianne said. "So, did you like him, Dana?"

"I did, and he got along fine with Bruno, which isn't always easy."

"Go on. Bruno is a sweetheart."

"Sometimes," Dana said, glancing at her watch. It was still early. Judy Porter and Teddy weren't due at the station until ten. "I'm going to take a quick walk over to the Pitman Gallery. Sam told me that Del came back last night and I want to talk to him."

Dana put her coat back on and wrapped her scarf around her head. She told Marianne to keep trying to get in touch with Casey and to call Bob too and remind them both of the staff meeting that afternoon.

"Will do," Marianne said. "How long will you be gone?"

"Not more than an hour," Dana answered. "I've got to sort through that mess on my desk before the meeting."

The sidewalks outside the newspaper building had been sanded and salted and Dana was wearing her fur-lined boots so the two-block walk to the gallery only took a few minutes.

Although the sign on the door said *Closed,* Del's car

was parked in the gallery's parking lot, so Dana was sure he was inside. She tapped on the window and Del came out of his office and opened the door for her.

"Good morning," Del said cheerfully. "It seems this is my day for unannounced visitors."

"Who else is here?" Dana asked softly.

"The love of your life."

"I'll come back later." Dana turned to go back outside, but she was too late. Bruno had come out of the office and seen her.

"Don't leave on my account," he said. "I'm about to question Del about his artist and I'm sure you're here for the same reason."

"Yes, please, Dana," Del said. "I've got a lot to catch up on, so let's combine the two questioning sessions."

Dana pulled the scarf from her head, feeling the static that made her curls fly around her face. She unbuttoned her coat as they all trouped into Del's office and sat down.

"Bruno already told me that Judy Porter and Teddy are being questioned this morning," Del said. "My first concern was whether she had legal counsel and Bruno said you arranged it, Dana. Thank you."

"You're welcome," Dana replied. She was puzzled by Del's casual attitude. "I still want to do whatever I can to help Judy."

"Okay," Bruno said. "Let's get down to it. Del, what do you know about Mrs. Porter's relationship with Teddy Larson?"

"They're friends," Del said. "She brought him over here to meet me one day and we all had lunch."

"You only met him once?"

"Yes. He's a very sweet boy, the son of Judy's neighbor, I believe."

"Other people I've questioned claim that he and Judy

were more than friends and that Judy's husband suspected something was going on between them. What do you know about that?"

"I know that Judy's husband was a lunkhead, but the girl loved him madly. She was so upset when he disappeared that she couldn't function. That's why I had to ask Dana to help her. Listen, Bruno, if you think Judy and Teddy had something to do with her husband's death, you're wrong. Those two are not bright enough or brave enough to kill a fly, much less a man like Lucas."

"I agree," Dana said.

Bruno turned and looked at her with a scowl, but said nothing. Dana glared back at him. Del got upset.

"Oh, my darlings," Del said. "Don't tell me you two are fighting again. I will never forgive myself if my asking Dana to help my artist drives a wedge between the two of you."

"I love Dana," Bruno said, still scowling. "I'd walk through fire for her, but sometimes I think she's only using me to get information and help on her cases. Her career means more to her than I do."

"This is still a pretty small town," Dana told him. "It's only natural that we'd become involved in the same cases. If it hadn't been for my career, we'd never have met in the first place."

"How true, how true," Del agreed quickly. "So, Bruno, if Judy is arrested will I be able to bail her out?"

"It depends on what she's charged with."

Del turned to Dana. "Will your paper be reporting on the fact that Judy is being questioned in connection with her husband's death?"

"I suppose so. We have two reporters who work the police beat and monitor what goes on at the station."

"Good."

"Good?" Bruno and Dana said together.

"I don't mean good that she's under suspicion. She's an innocent lamb, but the publicity would be good for the showing." Del tried not to smile, but his eyes reflected his good humor.

"If she's locked up in jail she won't be able to do much painting," Bruno told him.

Del sobered. "You need to look elsewhere for your killer, Bruno. My artist is not capable of murder."

"What about Judy's friend, Teddy?"

Del waved his hands in the air as if to clear the room of Bruno's suggestion. "Impossible."

Bruno stood up. "Killers come in all shapes, sizes and temperaments. Just because they don't look dangerous, doesn't mean they aren't. Lucas Porter abused his wife, which gives her a pretty strong motive."

Del looked at Dana, who had to agree that Bruno had a valid point. That coupled with the insurance policy just might send Judy Porter to prison.

Bruno sighed heavily and got to his feet. "Thanks for your time, Del. I'd better get back to the station." He put on the overcoat that hung from the back of his chair. "Are you going back to the paper?" Bruno asked Dana. "I came on foot, rather than try to skid along the icy streets in my car. I'll walk back with you."

"You go on," Dana told him. "I have another matter to discuss with Del."

"I'll bet," Bruno said. "I'll call you later."

Dana sat and waited while Del escorted Bruno to the door. He came back to the office smiling broadly.

"Okay, Del," Dana said. "What's going on? You seem very happy about a very sad turn of events."

"This is for your ears only, darling. Don't you dare share this information with Bruno. Promise me."

"I promise."

"Judy called me at 8:00 a.m. to tell me that she worked in her studio, ratty little room in her apartment actually, most of yesterday afternoon and all night. Didn't get a wink of sleep. She finished all the paintings I had contracted for and I went right over there and picked them all up. Come on, I'll show you."

Dana was stunned. "That's unbelievable."

"That was my first thought and I was also worried that they wouldn't be salable."

"Are they?"

"Judge for yourself."

Del stood up and Dana did the same. She followed him to a locked door down the hall from his office. Del quickly unlocked the door and allowed Dana to enter the room first. Judy Porter's paintings were the only ones in the room. The larger ones were leaning against the walls, the smaller ones were set out on a long worktable in the middle of the room.

Dana had seen most of them at Judy's apartment. They had been in various degrees of completion. She had never known anyone who worked on so many different pieces at the same time, and had marveled at Judy's ability to do so. She had also wondered if working on multiple pieces would diminish the final quality of the paintings. Now she could see for herself that Judy Porter's technique and work ethic had produced spectacular results.

"These are wonderful," Dana exclaimed as she walked around the room studying each painting.

"She is clearly one of the most talented young artists I've ever discovered," Del told her. "I hope I can count on you to keep her out of jail. A little adverse publicity will increase interest in the show, but I can't have my artist actually behind bars."

"Del, I can't stop Bruno from arresting her if he feels he has enough evidence to make the charges stick."

"Do you think he does?" he asked anxiously.

"I don't think he would have been here questioning you if he did."

"Good. Then all you have to do is use your influence with Bruno and convince him to look for other suspects."

Dana laughed. "You overestimate my powers of persuasion, Del. Bruno has a fit when I meddle in one of his cases. You just heard him voice his objections and we had an argument over that very thing last night."

"He seemed to want to make it up to you today," Del said.

"Only because his mother is coming for a visit soon and he wants me to help him entertain her."

"Bring her here. I'll take you both to lunch."

"You don't have to make rash promises, Del. I don't believe Judy Porter and Teddy Larson killed Lucas and I will keep working on the case. Based on the people I've already talked to, Lucas Porter had more enemies than friends."

"Judy told me she worked like a demon to complete the paintings because she couldn't bear the thought of leaving them unfinished while she was in prison."

"That sounds a lot like a confession to me."

"On the contrary, she swore to me that she was innocent, but she's terrified of Bruno."

"He has that effect on a lot of people," Dana replied.

ELEVEN

BY THE TIME THE STAFF meeting convened, Dana was more than a little worried about Casey. There had been no word from her all day and attempts to reach Casey on her home phone and cell phone had been unsuccessful.

"Do you think something could have happened to her?" Marianne asked Bob as they took seats in Dana's office.

"No. I'm sure she's okay. If there was a problem we would have heard something by now."

"You're probably right," Dana agreed. "It's just that it's so unlike Casey not to at least call in."

"She's never been in love before," Bob said. "Love makes people do all kinds of crazy things. Right, Marianne?"

Marianne smiled, but didn't answer him.

The outside door to the reception office opened and closed and all three of them look expectantly to the doorway of Dana's office expecting to see Casey cross the threshold. Instead, a strange man charged into the office.

Bob jumped up and confronted him. "Can I help you?" he said.

"I know you," the man shouted. "You're the fat guy that was with the skinny broad who brought her car in the other day. And yes, you can help me. I want a retraction and an apology for that pack of lies you printed about me and my garage."

Dana stood up. "Mr. Flannery?"

"Yeah, that's right," he acknowledged. "Who the hell are you?"

"I'm Dana Sloan, the head of Globe Investigations."

Flannery glared at her. He was a big man with a shaved head. His face was flushed with anger, his blue eyes bloodshot. He smelled of the whiskey he had already consumed that day. "Where's the skinny broad?" he asked. "That's who I want to talk to."

"She's not here," Bob told him.

"Please sit down, Mr. Flannery," Dana said calmly. "Marianne will get you a cup of coffee."

Marianne was already heading for the door to call security, but Flannery grabbed her arm as she tried to pass him. "Stay put, girlie," he ordered.

"Let go of her, please," Bob said in a soothing voice.

Flannery let go of Marianne's arm and took a swing at Bob. Although Bob was overweight, he was trained in martial arts. He deflected Flannery's punch and before the garage owner knew what happened, he found himself on the floor with the full weight of Bob's size-twelve foot pressing down on his back.

Marianne had quickly escaped to the outer office and called security. Flannery was yelling threats and obscenities but was unable to dislodge Bob's foot from the middle of his back.

Dana walked around and sat down in the chair Marianne had vacated so she could speak to the man on his level. "I understand that you're upset by the story we ran on your garage, but it was the result of several complaints we received. All of it is documented. Bursting in here, making threats and assaulting people is only going to make things worse for you, so I suggest you shut up and give me your lawyer's name. I'll call him so he can meet you at the police station."

The mention of the police station got Flannery's attention. "First you ruin my business and now you're going to have me arrested?"

Before Dana could answer two of the *Globe*'s uniformed security guards came into the office. Bob stepped aside as the two men hauled Flannery to his feet.

In the outer office, the telephone was ringing and Marianne answered it. "Globe Investigations." She paused and listened to the caller. "Casey, are you all right? We've been worried about you." Marianne listened to what Casey was telling her as Flannery was escorted out of the office. As the door closed behind him, Marianne said, "Hold on. Dana will want to hear this from you."

Bob danced around the office loosening up the muscles he had exerted subduing Flannery, while Dana hurried back to her desk and picked up the phone to talk to Casey.

"What's going on?" Dana asked.

"I'm sorry," Casey told her. "I meant to call earlier, but I got confused with the two-hour time difference. After we left you and Bruno last night, Tony whisked me off to the airport. We're in Las Vegas and we just got married."

"Wow," Dana said. "When you said you were thinking of getting married in Vegas, I didn't know you meant immediately."

Casey giggled. "Neither did I. It was all Tony's idea but to tell you the truth, I wasn't so keen on having a big wedding anyway. We'll be back in a week or so and we'll have a party to celebrate with all our friends at the country club. I hope it's all right that I take the time off for my honeymoon."

"You have plenty of time coming," Dana said. "I'm

really surprised by this, but I'm also really happy for you, Casey."

Bob was at Dana's side, wanting to grab the phone from her hand. "Let me talk to her," he said.

"Bob wants to say hello. I'll see you when you get back."

Dana let Bob take the phone while she rushed out to talk to Marianne, who was sitting behind her desk with her head in her hands.

"Are you all right?" Dana asked. "Did that jerk hurt you?"

Marianne straightened up and smiled. "I'm fine. No bruises. I just can't believe that Casey eloped to Las Vegas with a guy I've never even met."

"She sounded very happy on the phone," Dana said lamely.

Marianne nodded in agreement. The door to the hallway opened again and both girls turned to see Bruno filling the doorway.

"Hi, Bruno," Marianne said. "I'm glad it's you."

"I heard there was trouble here. Is everyone all right?"

"Yes, we're fine. Thanks to Bob," Dana told him.

"You're welcome," Bob said as he came out of Dana's office. "Did you hear the other news? Casey and her boyfriend eloped to Las Vegas."

Bruno's face registered his displeasure. "What?" he asked a little too loudly.

"They went to the airport after our dinner last night, flew to Vegas and got married this morning," Dana said. "What's wrong?"

"I need to talk to you, privately," Bruno replied. Noting the looks of alarm on the faces of Marianne and Bob, he quickly added, "It's about the Porter case."

"Oh, right. With everything that's been going on here, I forgot about that," Dana said. "Come on. I want the details."

She turned and walked into her office and Bruno followed, shutting the door behind him. Bob and Marianne looked at each other and smiled.

"I'm going to see if I can scare up some doughnuts. You want one?" Bob asked Marianne.

"Yes. One with lots of chocolate frosting, please. I'll make a fresh pot of coffee."

Inside Dana's office, Bruno took off his topcoat and threw it across one of the chairs while he sank wearily into the other one. Dana, feeling that bad news was coming, walked behind her desk, sat down and folded her hands on top of the desk. "Okay. Give it to me straight," she told Bruno. "Did you arrest Judy Porter?"

Bruno shook his head. "No. I still like her for the deed, but Teddy's mother swears that she was with both of them the night Lucas disappeared. We had to let them go until I can prove that the mother is lying to protect them."

Dana sighed. "I'm sorry if you're upset about that, Bruno, but I still don't think—"

"That's not what I'm upset about. From everything I've learned whoever killed Lucas Porter did the world a favor. I'm still going to find out who did it and bring him or her or them to justice, but that's not what I'm upset about. It's Casey running off and marrying Hunter."

Dana sucked in a breath. "Why? What did you find out?"

"I ran his fingerprints through the database. The reason Hunter's existence only began two years ago is because that's when he got out of prison and got a Social Security card and began to live in the real world."

"He must have gone to jail as a juvenile," Dana said.

"That's right. He was sixteen, but they tried him as an adult."

Dana forced herself to ask the next question although she was already pretty sure she didn't want to hear the answer. "What did he do?"

"He and his older brother held up a bank. They got a bundle of money and took a woman hostage to ensure their getaway. The woman was found dead a few hours later. Eventually, the Hunter boys were arrested but the money was never recovered. They claimed the woman's death was an accident, but they both got twenty-five years to life. His brother is still in prison, but Tony was a model prisoner and got out early for good behavior."

Bruno stopped talking and let Dana digest the information he was giving her. Her hazel eyes turned to brown as the thoughts she was having darkened them.

"Where did this happen?"

"In Chicago."

"He seemed a little concerned last night when he found out you were a cop. Do you think that's why he rushed Casey off to Vegas to get married?"

"That's exactly what I think," Bruno said solemnly.

Dana leaned back in her chair. "Do you think that Casey could be in danger?"

"I don't know. I do know that he's probably not really a rich guy. There's no record of him working the last two years so his money may be running out by now. Three hundred thousand dollars doesn't go as far as it would have twenty years ago."

"Weren't the Chicago police watching him when he got out of jail to see if he went to get the missing money?"

Bruno laughed softly. "In a big city like Chicago, guys

like Hunter just fall through the cracks. No one would even remember the case or the fact that the money was never recovered."

"Right," Dana agreed. "Oh God, Bruno. What am I going to do? Casey sounded so happy on the phone. This will destroy her."

"No one says you have to tell her."

Dana jumped to her feet. "And let her be married to a criminal? A murderer?"

Bruno got up and walked over to Dana. He put his arms around her and held her close. "Listen, sweets, Hunter was a kid when the crime happened. As far as we know, he's stayed out of trouble since being released from prison."

"Except for using stolen money to live on," Dana said.

"Except for that. But after spending all those years in jail, the guy probably felt he'd paid his debt to society and the money was his to keep."

Another thought struck Dana and she pulled away from Bruno. "What if his money is running out and that's why he married Casey? He could be after her money."

"How much does she have?"

"I don't know, but when she gets back to town, I'm going to find out."

"Are you going to tell her about Hunter's past?"

Dana's eyes filled with tears and she let Bruno pull her close again. "I'm hoping she already knows."

"You think that Casey would have married him if she knew?"

"Maybe. It's like Bob said just before Flannery came bursting in here. He said that Casey has never been in love before and women in love do all kinds of crazy things."

"Except for you," Bruno said. "I keep hoping but…"

Dana smiled in spite of her concern for Casey. "Don't lose hope, big guy," she replied.

TWELVE

THE VERY NEXT DAY, Del decided that he had better push up the date for Judy Porter's showing just in case Bruno was able to break her alibi.

"I still don't think Judy is guilty," Del told Dana when he called to tell her that the show was scheduled for the next Saturday. "But just to be on the safe side I've switched Judy's showing with another artist."

"I'm sorry, Del. With Casey still off on her honeymoon, we're shorthanded and I haven't had time to look into any more leads on the Porter case."

"It's okay, darling. To be honest, the continued publicity the case is getting has stirred more than the usual interest in Judy's showing."

"And if I were to be honest, I'd have to admit that I really don't have any leads to look into at the moment."

"Will you be bringing Bruno to the showing?"

"Not if it will make Judy uncomfortable."

"It would make Judy uncomfortable."

"He'll probably have to work anyway. With his mother coming for a visit soon, he's trying to clear his desk so he can spend more time with her."

"All right, darling. I'll see you Saturday."

Dana hung up hoping that Bruno would indeed have to work on Saturday night so she wouldn't have to tell him he couldn't come to the gallery with her.

A few minutes later, Marianne came in to tell Dana that she was wanted in Sam McGowan's office.

Dana had been looking at a file on a new case involving an apartment complex in Pine Grove City. One of the tenants had called the paper and reported that her landlady was hiding aliens in an empty apartment in the basement. Bob had gone over to speak to the woman thinking that she was referring to illegal aliens from another country. Instead the woman claimed the aliens were from another planet. Bob's report was quite amusing as he described his trek into the basement to look for the aliens, but Dana would have to finish reading it later.

A man Dana had never seen before was already seated in Sam's office when Dana came through the door. Both men rose and Sam introduced Dana to Benjamin Hughes, who turned out to be Floyd Flannery's lawyer.

"I'm sorry to meet you under these adverse circumstances," Hughes said as he shook Dana's hand. "I understand my client caused a scene in your office yesterday."

"To put it mildly," Dana replied.

Hughes waited until Dana was seated before he sat down again. Sam hadn't budged from his chair and Dana knew he was probably getting impatient for the meeting to begin.

"Mr. Hughes has a deal he wants to make with us," Sam said.

"Yes. My client is very sorry for yesterday's incident and sends his sincere apologies."

"Did he spend the night in jail?"

"Yes. By the time all the paperwork was processed, it was too late for a bail hearing."

"So he sobered up and sent you here to get us to drop the charges against him," Sam said impatiently.

"Mr. Flannery still feels that your paper slandered him and caused irreparable harm to his business. However, in light of his lack of good judgment yesterday, he has decided not to proceed with the lawsuit providing that your newspaper and staff members will drop the charges against him."

"We received several complaints about Mr. Flannery's business practices," Dana said firmly. "Our investigation proved that the complaints were valid and that's what we reported. You client doesn't have a case."

Benjamin Hughes smiled at Dana. "You have a very good reputation, Miss Sloan. I'm actually a big fan of yours, but please consider the time, energy and money that will be expended on a lawsuit."

Dana turned to her editor. "It's Sam's call."

"I'll talk to our lawyer and get back to you," Sam said curtly. "Thanks for stopping by."

Sam's obvious attempt at dismissal didn't seem to affect Hughes, who remained seated. "I really hope we can come to an agreement on this. Mr. Flannery is a decent, hard-working man and—"

Sam stood up. "Mr. Hughes, I don't take kindly to people who threaten my staff and if you want my answer to your proposition, it's no. However, I will present it to the *Globe*'s legal advisors. You'll hear from them directly."

The lawyer reluctantly got to his feet, nodded to Dana and left the office. After he was gone, Sam sat down again and waited to Dana to voice her opinion.

"It seems rather odd for Hughes to come to us directly," Dana said. "Why didn't he just speak to our lawyers?"

"He probably has already and didn't get anywhere so he came to me hoping I'd go along with his plan."

"Maybe we'd better do a background check on Flannery and see if he could be truly dangerous," Dana suggested.

"I've already got that in the works," Sam told her. "Did Del call you about Judy Porter's art show?"

"Yes. I assume you and Emily are going?"

"I'm afraid so. I hope Bruno is going to be there."

"Sorry," Dana said. "He doesn't like the shows any more than you do, and Del would prefer he not be there to make his artist uncomfortable."

"I can understand that. Did you learn anything new on the case?"

"I haven't had time to work on it with Casey on her honeymoon. Fortunately for Judy Porter, Bruno hasn't uncovered any new incriminating evidence, either."

"When is Casey coming back?"

"Friday night, I think. I'm hoping to have a chance to talk to her Saturday before the art show."

"Did Bruno check out the new husband for you?"

Dana nodded. "He did, and that's what I need to speak to Casey about."

Sam cocked his head to one side. "Sounds serious."

"Maybe not," Dana said brightly. She stood up. "I'd better get back to the office."

Sam stood up and walked her to the door. "I guess you don't want to tell me what Bruno found out."

"No, I don't," Dana answered honestly. "Not before I talk to Casey about it."

Sam accepted her answer and watched Dana hurry out of his office and across the newsroom like she couldn't wait to put distance between them.

A FEW BLOCKS AWAY, Floyd Flannery and Ben Hughes were leaving the courthouse.

"My wife didn't even show up for the hearing," Floyd complained to his lawyer. "She's probably had the locks on the house changed already."

"Janine is upset," Ben told him. "This isn't the first time she's had to bail you out. She had to go to her brother for the money she needed for the bondsman."

"She could have put the house up for collateral. That's what she did the last time."

"I advised her not to do that," Ben told him calmly.

Floyd's face flushed with anger. "Why the hell would you do that?"

Ben stopped walking and faced his irate client. "Because you're in big trouble this time, Floyd. I talked to the lawyers for the *Globe* and they're not going to make a deal. There's going to be a trial and you may go to prison. Janine is going to need the equity in your house for your legal bills and her living expenses."

"It's all that reporter's fault. So what if I told people they needed extra work on their cars? The stuff I replaced needed replacing. Since that story came out in the paper, my business has gone right in the toilet."

Ben looked at his watch. "Don't blame anyone else for your problems, Floyd. The reporter was just following up on the complaints they got about you."

"If I ever catch up with that broad…"

"Shut up, Floyd. You're not going to do anything but go home and stay there."

"And if I don't?" Flannery asked belligerently.

"You'll be back in jail and using a public defender."

Hughes turned and walked away, leaving his client standing on the street corner shaking with rage.

THIRTEEN

CASEY WOKE UP EARLY and ventured into Tony's kitchen.
Their flight from Las Vegas had gotten in at 8:00 p.m. the
night before. From the airport they had gone to Casey's
mom's house. Nina Jordan had greeted them rather coolly.
She was obviously upset that her only daughter had chosen
to elope rather than let Nina have the pleasure of planning
a nice wedding.

Casey smiled as she remembered how Tony had refused
to be put off by Nina's attitude and outdid himself in the
charm department. They took Nina to dinner and by dessert
she was beaming at her new son-in-law, her disappointment
about the way they had gotten married forgotten. Nina had
quickly convinced herself that the most important thing
was that Casey had found herself a wealthy husband and
would never again have to struggle financially the way
Nina had.

Strangely enough, Nina Jordan had never questioned
her daughter's sudden progression into the elite world of
the country club set. She was elated to see Casey shed
her old image and take an active interest in fashionable
clothes, modern hairstyles and beauty products. When
Casey brought Tony home to meet her for the first time,
Nina thought all the dreams she had secretly harbored for
Casey were going to come true.

Nina had divorced Casey's father shortly after the birth
of her daughter and he had promptly disappeared. It had

been hard to raise a child on her own, but she had done her best and Casey's natural wit and intelligence had done the rest.

After dinner, Tony and Casey stopped by Casey's apartment so she could pack some clothes to bring to Tony's place. Her lease on the apartment was up the end of March and she would give her landlord a thirty-day notice that she was not renewing it. Tony's apartment was larger and had recently been renovated, so that's where they would live for the time being.

Tony kept talking about her quitting her job at the *Globe* and staying home to have babies. Of course Tony was still under the impression that the inheritance that enabled Casey to join Crescent Hills Country Club was large enough that she didn't need to work.

The three Cs had thought ahead to the end of the master plan and come up with a story that Casey could use to explain the evaporation of her wealth once Prince Charming had fallen in love with her.

Casey was supposed to say, "The bulk of my uncle's estate was invested in a pyramid scheme that has now collapsed. I'm broke again."

If Tony started asking questions about the pyramid scheme, Casey was supposed to start crying and say that she didn't have any details. All she knew for sure was that the money had suddenly vanished.

Although Casey had imagined the scenario dozens of times, she never actually had the courage to broach the subject with Tony. It was just another lie to add to the larger deception that had allowed her to attract Tony in the first place.

Casey found a can of coffee in one of the cabinets and soon had a pot of coffee brewing. However, the refrigerator was barren and so was the pantry and every other place Casey looked for food.

Taking up a place at the window that looked out over a walled courtyard, Casey hugged herself. Marriage should be based on mutual trust and honesty and she would find the right time to tell Tony the truth about herself and her financial assets. If he truly loved her, and she believed that he did, it wouldn't matter how they had come to know each other and fallen in love.

"Hey, the coffee smells wonderful," Tony said as he appeared in the doorway to the kitchen. Casey spun around, startled out of the thoughts and doubts that haunted her.

"Good morning," she said, crossing the room to walk into his arms.

"Good morning. What are we going to do with this fine day?"

"Well, first of all, I think we need to go grocery shopping. Your cupboards are bare."

Tony laughed. "That's why I married you. I can't cook and don't know the first thing about grocery shopping."

"I'll teach you everything I know," she promised.

A few hours later, they had breakfast in the deli section of Sunflower Market. Ham-and-cheese quiche with sliced fruit was served on plastic plates.

George came out of the storeroom pushing a hand truck loaded with produce cartons. "Hi, George," Casey called out. Like Dana, Casey shopped at the Sunflower on a regular basis and was acquainted with George.

George stopped and waved at Casey. Then, he noticed Tony sitting across from her and walked over with a curious expression on his weathered face. "Who's this guy?" George asked. "I thought you were my girl?"

Casey laughed. "This is my brand-new husband, Tony

Hunter. Tony, meet my friend George. Gee, George, I'm sorry I don't know your last name."

"Last names are not important here," George said, reaching across the table to shake hands with Tony. "You're a lucky man, Tony Hunter. Casey is a beautiful person."

"I know it," Tony said. "It's nice to meet you."

"So, are you kids going to be living in the neighborhood?"

"For a while," Casey answered. "Tony has an apartment in the Rialto building on Sixteenth Street."

"Don't know the place," George admitted. "Well, I'd better get this lettuce put up before the big rush starts. My good wishes to you both."

George hurried off to the produce department guiding the hand truck expertly through the aisles that were already beginning to fill up with Saturday-morning shoppers.

By the time Tony and Casey finished their breakfast and got to the produce department George had finished filling the lettuce bins. They heard his name announced over the store's intercom system. George was needed at checkout stand number three.

"Bagging groceries is George's favorite job. He always insists on helping the ladies to their cars with their groceries," Casey said.

Tony was studying a bag of corn chips and not really listening to Casey. "What about these?" he said, turning to Casey. "It says they're low in fat and salt."

"And taste," Casey told him. "Get the brand-name on the top shelf."

Finally, their cart was loaded with groceries and Tony pushed it to the checkout lanes. As he was unloading their purchases to be checked out, Casey saw Carmen enter the store and called out to her.

Carmen came rushing over. "Where have you been?"

she asked breathlessly. "I've been calling you for days at home and on your cell. You didn't answer either."

"I know. I haven't had a chance to return my calls yet. I've been in Las Vegas with Tony." Casey paused dramatically. "We got married."

Carmen let out a big squeal and hugged Casey. Tony turned around to see what was going on. "Oh, hi, Carmen. How are you?"

"I'm great and I'm so happy for you two. I can't believe you did it. How exciting is that?"

Tony smiled and nodded at her patiently, and then turned back to the cashier, who was still ringing up all the groceries they had purchased.

Carmen and Casey chatted for another few minutes and then Carmen said she had to work this morning and just stopped by to pick up doughnuts for the office staff.

"It's Saturday," Casey said.

"I know but the bigwigs are coming here from Chicago on Monday and the boss wants the office in primo condition. Call me later," Carmen said giving Casey another quick hug.

"That will be $210.53," the checkout lady said to Tony as Casey turned back to see the groceries had all been bagged and stacked back into the cart.

Tony looked at his wife. "Honey, I forgot my wallet. You'll have to pay the bill."

Casey tried not to show her alarm, she had no cash and her checking account had less than $50 in it. She knew that Tony didn't use credit cards and the one she had in her purse was close to being maxed out. She had used it in Las Vegas to buy the dress she had been married in.

"I'll have to write a check," Casey finally said. The bank would be closed today and Casey would have to go

there first thing Monday morning to cover it. She took
out her checkbook and started writing the check, hoping
that Sunflower Market didn't have one of those electronic
terminals that accessed the bank account to make sure
there were sufficient funds to cover customers' personal
checks.

Casey held her breath as the cashier processed the check
and let it out when the woman smiled and handed her the
receipt and wished them a good day.

Casey relaxed some as she and Tony unloaded the groceries into the back of his Cadillac Escalade. Tony's vehicle
was top of the line with all the bells and whistles. She
didn't have to worry about money any longer; she had married a wealthy man. *Under false pretenses,* her conscience
chided.

Casey was silent on the short drive back to the apartment, worrying about the conversation she needed to have
with her new husband.

"What's wrong, Casey?" Tony finally asked when
they were back in his kitchen putting the groceries away.
"You've been awfully quiet since we left the store."

"Nothing," Casey replied. "I'm just stunned that we
spent so much at the store, and we still have empty shelves
in your pantry."

"Since when do you have to worry about things like
that?" he asked.

"I haven't always had money," Casey said. "I inherited
what I have and—" She stopped. "Oh, never mind. I don't
want to talk about it now."

Tony looked at her with a frown. "Are you mad because
I forgot my wallet and you had to pay for the groceries?"
he asked sharply.

"No, of course not," she said quickly.

"Good, because a lot of my funds are tied up right now and you may have to pay some of the bills until the market adjusts itself."

Casey stopped with her hand on the freezer handle and a bag of frozen corn in midair. Tony was using the line she was supposed to use on him. She quickly opened the freezer and was grateful for the cold air that hit her burning cheeks as she placed the frozen corn inside.

When she finally closed the freezer door and turned around to face Tony, he was staring at her. His frown had turned to suspicion as he waited for her to comment on his last statement.

"Tony, darling," Casey said softly. "Maybe we'd better sit down and talk about our finances."

"Why? Is paying a few bills going to be a problem for you?"

Casey didn't answer. She walked swiftly out of the kitchen into the living room and sat down on the leather sofa that occupied one whole wall.

Tony's apartment was filled with expensive furniture, but the walls and mahogany tables were empty. No artwork, no family photos and no travel mementos to make the rooms comfortable and homey.

In the middle of the living room floor, Tony had set up an electronic golf contraption so he could practice his putting while he waited for the frozen greens at the country club to thaw.

Tony came into the room and pulled a putter out of the golf bag that stood next to his practice equipment. He deftly stroked a golf ball setting at the end of the artificial strip of green and watched the ball sink into the plastic cup at the other end.

"Tony, please sit down here. I want to talk to you."

Tony sighed and leaned the putter against his golf bag. He walked over and sat down on the sofa next to Casey.

"Okay, darling. What do you want to tell me?"

"Something I should have told you long ago. I haven't been completely honest with you. I love you, Tony, and I hope you'll listen with your heart and see how sorry I am that I didn't tell you before now."

Tony smiled at her and took her hand. "Come on, Casey. I love you too. You're my wife now. There's nothing you can say that will make me think badly of you."

FOURTEEN

INSPIRED BY THE THOUGHT of Judy Porter's art show that evening, Dana got up early and painted. If Judy Porter could finish seven or eight paintings in twenty-four hours, Dana told herself that she could surely finish the one piece she'd been laboring over for months.

The painting was a scene that was very dear to Dana's heart, and perhaps that's why she was having so much trouble finishing it. She wanted to get it perfect.

The farm where Dana had grown up had changed a lot over the years as it became more modern and mechanized. That was fine and good for her family, who still lived there, worked the land and tended the animals, but Dana wanted to capture the images she had from her childhood on the canvas.

At one time in her life, Dana had been sure she would become a professional artist. She had always loved to draw and paint and everyone said she was very talented. It was while she was pursuing an art degree in college that Dana suddenly altered her career path.

When Dana was in her second year at the University of Illinois, she began dating the editor of the college paper. Craig talked her into helping out at the paper so they could spend more time together. Dana liked the newspaper office and the creative aspects of putting the paper together.

Soon she was helping Craig chase down stories and write copy. The next semester, Dana changed her major to journalism and had been working in the field ever since, letting her art become a part-time hobby.

The doorbell rang and Dana put down her brush and went to answer it. Bruno had called earlier and said he would be working all day and half the night, so she knew it wasn't him.

Dana opened the door and found Casey standing there wearing a pair of dark glasses. "Hi, Dana. I'm sorry to show up unannounced, but I need to talk to you."

Dana pulled her inside and hugged her. "I'm really glad to see you. I wasn't sure what time you were getting back."

Casey was trembling and Dana knew immediately that something was wrong. She pushed the door closed and led Casey to the sofa and sat her down.

Casey shrugged out of the coat she was wearing and took off her dark glasses. Her eyes were red and puffy and when she read the look of concern on Dana's face, she began to cry again.

A few days ago, Casey seemed to be the happiest girl on earth and now she was a wreck. Given the information Bruno had given her about Tony Hunter, Dana's concern for her friend was escalating into cold hard fear.

"What's wrong, Casey?" Dana said firmly. "Has something happened between you and Tony?"

Casey nodded and began wiping her face and nose with a tissue. Dana reached behind her and handed Casey the box she kept on the end table next to the sofa.

"I'm sorry. I didn't mean to fall apart like this," Casey muttered.

"Just tell me what happened," Dana said. "Did he hurt you?"

"Tony wants a divorce."

"A divorce? You haven't even been married a week."

"I know, but I've been deceiving him from the beginning and now that he knows the truth he doesn't want me anymore. I thought he loved me. I thought he would understand."

Dana was struggling to make sense of what Casey was saying. "I have no idea what you're talking about, Casey. You'd better start at the beginning and tell me everything."

Casey nodded and took a deep breath. "We got back last night and went to see my mom. Then we went to my place and I packed up most of my clothes and we moved everything over to Tony's apartment. Everything was wonderful. I was so happy."

"Okay," Dana said slowly. "Then what happened?"

"This morning, I discovered that Tony had nothing in the house to eat, so I suggested that we go to the grocery store. We got in his car and drove over to Sunflower Market. It's close to Tony's place. That's where we saw Carmen."

"Who's Carmen?"

"My girlfriend. We went to high school together and were roommates at college. Anyway, she was very excited when I told her Tony and I had just gotten married. We were at the checkout counter and the girl was ringing up our groceries. Then, Tony discovered he hadn't brought his wallet with him to pay for all the groceries we bought. I had my checkbook with me, so I wrote a check for the groceries and we went home. I was upset because I knew there wasn't enough money in my account to cover the check I wrote."

"Your paycheck is at the office," Dana told her. "If it will help we can go over and pick it up so you can put it in the bank right away."

"I know, but Tony saw that I was upset and we started

talking about our finances and I broke down and told him about the master plan."

Now Dana was really confused. "The master plan," she repeated. "What on earth is that?"

"It's a crazy, stupid thing Carmen and I and Cathy thought up one night."

"Tell me about it," Dana said.

"It's really embarrassing."

"I don't care, Casey," Dana told her. "I can't help you if I don't know the whole story."

Casey nodded and told Dana about the scheme she and her two friends had devised to meet and marry rich husbands. When she was finished, Dana got up and began to pace.

"That's a pretty dramatic twist," Dana said, trying not to sound too judgmental. "All this time you've been trying to check Tony out to make sure he was who he appeared to be, while you were pretending to be somebody you're not."

"I told you it was embarassing," Casey said. "But as crazy as it sounds, it actually worked. I met Tony and Carmen is dating his golfing buddy, Fred, and Cathy is hot and heavy with the club's tennis pro."

"All three of you are nuts," Dana exclaimed. "Do the guys Carmen and Cathy are dating know about the plan?"

"No, but it doesn't matter. Fred and what's his name know the girls came to the club as my guests and have accepted the fact that they aren't rich, like I'm supposed to be."

"It seems to me that you took all the risks, Casey."

"I knew that up front. I guess I should have told Tony the truth from the beginning. I'm sure it's the fact that

I've been lying to him since we met that really made him angry."

"What if you found out that Tony had been lying to you too?"

"I love him, Dana. I would forgive him and I thought he felt the same about me. I guess it's just as well he found out now. I couldn't keep up the pretense much longer. He's been telling me I should quit my job so we could have children. That and the way he spends money convinced me he had enough money for us to live on without me ever having to work again."

"All right," Dana said. "So you told Tony that you're actually a poor working girl and he reacted badly."

"He literally threw me out of his apartment. He said I was nothing but a gold digger and he never wanted to see me again." Dana thought Casey might start crying again, but she squared her shoulders and tossed her head defiantly. "Well, you know what? He is going to see me again. I have to go back there and get my things." Casey stood up and grabbed at her coat. "Will you come with me?"

"Hold on, Casey," Dana said. "You confessed your scheme to Tony, but I take it you still don't know anything about his background."

"No, I don't, and at this point, I don't care. I think he married me for the money he thought I had, which means he's not what he seems to be, either. Boy, that would be the real twist."

"Yes, it will be," Dana said softly. "Put your coat down, Casey. I'm going to make a pot of coffee. You and I have a lot more to talk about."

DANA HAD INVITED Marianne to come to the gallery showing that evening. Marianne's boyfriend, Greg, was at a seminar in Chicago. Greg was a policeman turned social worker who worked with teenagers trying to keep them out of trouble and harm's way.

Marianne had offered to drive to the gallery because she had a vehicle with four-wheel drive and they were predicting more snow for that evening. She picked Dana up at 7:30 p.m. The first thing Marianne asked when Dana got into the Jeep was whether she had heard from Casey.

"Yes, as a matter of fact, she came by earlier today," Dana said carefully.

"So, how's she doing?"

"She's okay," Dana lied. "I'm sure she'll want to tell you everything herself when she comes back to the office on Monday."

Marianne stopped at a traffic light and turned to look at Dana, who was casually gazing out her window. "I'll bet Casey is just glowing, isn't she?"

"Not exactly," Dana replied, not wanting to give Marianne the details, but not wanting to mislead her either.

"Is something wrong?"

"Nothing earth-shattering," Dana replied. "She and Tony had a squabble, but I'm sure they've worked things out by now."

"Oh, I see," Marianne said smugly. "It's probably just a lover's quarrel. All couples go through that."

Dana laughed. "Bruno and I have one almost every day."

"Greg and I had one on our third date, but we kissed and made up and things have been great ever since."

"What kind of seminar is he attending in Chicago?" Dana asked. She was grateful to have been able to maneuver the subject away from Casey. Dana could still see the stunned expression and the hurt in Casey's eyes when Dana told her what Bruno had uncovered about Tony Hunter.

"No wonder we could only trace him back a few years," Casey had finally said. "That's when he got out of prison."

Casey's shock had quickly turned to anger as she realized the secrets that Tony had been keeping from her were a lot more serious than the one she had been keeping from him.

"How could I have been so stupid?" Casey said, jumping off the stool she had been sitting on at Dana's kitchen counter. "I've been an investigator for almost five years; I know better."

"Don't be too hard on yourself, Casey," Dana had told her. "You fell in love and love makes us want to believe the best about our partner."

"And he had the nerve to call me a gold digger," Casey said softly. "He's a thief and a murderer. I'll bet that money he's been throwing around is from the bank he robbed."

It took Dana more than an hour to get Casey calmed down. Finally, she got Casey to agree that she should not confront Tony until she took some time to think everything through. Casey left Dana's apartment, promising to go to her own apartment to think things through.

"I'm going to the show at Pitman Gallery," Dana told her friend. "Call me on my cell phone if you need me."

As Marianne chattered on about Greg and the work he was doing with teenagers, Dana's cell phone rang.

"Excuse me," Dana said as she pulled the phone out of her purse and answered it.

"Hi, sweets. Where are you?" Bruno said cheerfully.

"I'm with Marianne. We're on the way to Judy Porter's show at the gallery."

"Oh, yeah. The one I'm not invited to attend."

"That's right," Dana replied. "You're working, remember?"

"Yes, I am, and I'm making some real progress tonight."

"Really? On what case?"

"Can't tell you, honey. I'll be done about nine. I thought I'd drop by the gallery and pick you up."

"Okay, but promise me you'll wait for me in the parking lot. I don't want you coming inside and upsetting Judy. This is a big night for her and for Del too."

"It may turn out to be bigger than she expected."

"What does that mean?"

"I've got another call. I'll see you later."

Bruno hung up and Dana stared at her phone. "He's going to cause trouble," she said instinctively.

"For Judy Porter?" Marianne asked.

"I think so."

"Uh-oh. Do you think he's found some new evidence?"

"Probably. He was much too cheerful."

"Are you going to warn Del?"

"No. It would just upset him."

Marianne drove into the parking lot of the gallery. It was already filled with cars. "There's Sam's car," she said.

"Good. He and Emily can help us with Del if Bruno comes in and spoils the party."

The gallery was filled with people that Dana and Marianne often read about in the *Globe*'s social pages. Del Pitman had a golden reputation and the elite of Crescent Hills always turned up for his parties.

Dana looked around, wondering how many people in the crowd were members of Crescent Hills Country Club and knew Tony and Casey. Dana was worried about Casey and what was going to happen between her investigator and her new husband. Then, Dana spotted Judy Porter standing in the middle of the exhibit room, meeting and greeting the people who had come to view her paintings. The artist looked like she had just stepped out of a Swiss village with blond braids piled on top of her head and a long white dress embroidered with colorful flowers. Her friend Teddy was hovering close behind her. Dressed in a tuxedo, Teddy looked taller and more confident than he had when Dana had first met him.

"What a mess," Dana muttered.

"What?" Marianne asked.

"Nothing. Let's find Sam and Emily," Dana suggested.

"I want to look at the paintings first," Marianne said. "I'll catch up with you at the buffet table. I'm sure that's where Sam is hanging out."

"I'd better say hello to Judy first," Dana decided. "Come on, I'll introduce you."

Judy Porter greeted Dana with a hug. "I'm so glad you're here," she whispered in Dana's ear. "I'm a nervous wreck." Dana introduced the artist to Marianne, who said hello and then quickly moved off to look at the art display.

Teddy came up to Judy and Dana. "Hi, Teddy," Dana said, offering her hand.

"Hi, Miss Sloan. It's nice to see you again."

"Is your mother here?" Dana asked.

"No. She said she didn't have the proper clothes to mingle with the rich folks. My suit is rented."

Dana smiled at his boyish honesty. "You look very nice."

Another couple came up to talk to Judy, so Dana excused herself and went to find Sam. As Marianne had predicted, he was standing next to the buffet table with a plate of canapés in each hand.

"Are you extra hungry?" Dana asked, taking a place next to him.

"Here," he offered one of the plates to Dana. "Emily took off again and I can't eat my food while I'm holding hers. She can get her own when she comes back."

Dana shrugged and popped one of the canapés in her mouth. It was a cracker with some kind of gooey cheese on top of it. "Thanks. I'm starving," she said as she followed the cracker with a mushroom she dipped in ranch dressing. "How's it going?"

"You know how I feel about these things. Where's Bruno?" In the past, Sam and Bruno had found a corner where they could talk sports while Emily and Dana enjoyed the artwork.

"He's working, but he hinted that he might show up here and I think it may have something to do with the Porter case."

"New evidence?"

"That's what he hinted at on the phone. I was thinking that maybe you could watch for him and talk him into waiting until the show is over before he makes a scene."

Sam laughed softly. "Dana, you're the only one who has any influence over Detective Al Bruno."

"Then I guess there's going to be a scene." Dana's cell phone rang again. "I hope this isn't him," she said as she clicked the phone on. It wasn't Bruno. It was Casey and she was hysterical. "Casey, slow down. I can't understand you."

"He's dead," Casey sobbed. "Tony is dead."

FIFTEEN

SAM AND DANA ARRIVED at Tony Hunter's apartment and found Casey standing outside waiting for them. She was shivering and it wasn't entirely due to the cold February air.

"Have you called the police?" Sam asked.

Casey shook her head in a negative response. Dana thought Casey looked bad when she had shown up at her apartment that morning, and thought she looked worse after Dana had told her about Tony's past, but that was nothing compared to the way she appeared now.

"I'm afraid she may go into shock," Dana said to Sam. "Let's get her inside."

Sam and Dana brought Casey inside the building. Tony's apartment was one of two on the first floor and Dana saw that the door was standing open. As they approached the doorway, Casey stiffened.

"I can't," she whispered hoarsely.

There was a stairway leading to another pair of apartments on the second floor of the building. "I'll stay here with Casey," Dana told Sam. "You go in and see what happened."

Sam helped Dana sit Casey down on one of the lower steps and then hurried toward the doorway. Within a few seconds, Sam was back.

"Call Bruno on his cell phone," he instructed. Sam's

tone of voice and his request for Bruno left no doubt that Tony Hunter's death was neither natural nor accidental.

Casey sat motionless, staring straight ahead. Dana stood up and Sam took her place on the stairs next to Casey. He put his arm around her, but she didn't seem to notice.

Dana walked outside. Bruno's cell phone number was on speed dial on Dana's phone. He answered on the first ring.

"I'm at the gallery," Bruno said. "Where are you?"

Dana quickly explained the emergency that had called her and Sam to Casey's side and gave him the address. He promised to be there in ten minutes. "I think we need the paramedics for Casey," Dana told him. "She's really a mess."

The paramedics arrived before Bruno. They took one look at Casey and hustled her off to their vehicle to check her vital signs. That gave Dana a chance to ask Sam how bad the death scene was.

"He's in the living room with a rather large hole in the middle of his forehead. There's a golf club on the floor next to him. That's really all I could see from the doorway and I didn't want to try and get a closer look and contaminate the scene."

They heard the squeal of tires outside and saw the flashing light that Bruno put on top of his car when he needed to get somewhere fast. In another minute, Bruno's linebacker body was filling up the space in the hallway.

Bruno put his hands on Dana's shoulders and gazed into her eyes. "Are you okay?" he asked.

"I'm fine."

"I took a look from Hunter's doorway," Sam told him. "He's on the living room floor with a golf club next to him. He was shot in the head."

"Anyone else go inside the apartment?"

"Casey probably did," Dana said. "But she's in no condition to be questioned right now."

"The lab guys are on their way," Bruno said as he walked away.

When Bruno was out of earshot, Sam spoke quietly to Dana. "Why don't you go out and check on Casey? I'll hang around here on the chance this turns into a bigger story than I think it's going to be."

Dana nodded and walked out into the frigid night air again. The back door to the paramedic van was open and Dana could see Casey sitting inside with one of the attendants talking to her. Some of the color had returned to Casey's face, but Dana didn't know if she was feeling better or whether the cold air was responsible for the flush that had returned to her cheeks.

As Dana walked closer the paramedic got out of the vehicle and met her halfway. "Your friend is still pretty shook-up, but I don't think she needs to go to the hospital. Why don't you go and talk to her while I round up my partner?"

Dana climbed into the vehicle and sat down next to Casey. "How are you doing?"

"According to my vitals, I'm not going to have a stroke or even pass out. I saw Bruno go into the building. I'd better pull myself together. I'm sure he'll want to question me."

"He's busy at the moment. Can you tell me what happened?"

Casey nodded. "After I left you, I went back to my apartment and Floyd Flannery was sitting out in front waiting for me."

"Oh, no," Dana said. "He came to the office last week and threatened us. Bob had to knock him down and we had him arrested. Someone must have bailed him out."

"I didn't know that," Casey told her.

"I should have told you this afternoon, but I forgot all about him. What happened with him?"

"We got into an argument about my investigation of his garage and all the problems it had caused for him. I was so upset over Tony that I just lost it and started screaming at him. The people who live downstairs from me came out to see if I was in trouble and Flannery ran off."

"Flannery is a loose cannon," Dana said. "He belongs behind bars."

Casey took a deep breath and closed her eyes. "Do you think he could have come here and killed Tony to get even with me? Oh my God. It could be my fault Tony is dead."

After the way Flannery had acted in her office, Dana thought it was a possibility, but for Casey's sake, she quickly denied it. "How would he have known where Tony lived? No, it's impossible. Nothing you have ever done or said could have caused this to happen to Tony. So Flannery ran off and then what did you do?"

"I went upstairs and called Carmen and Cathy and told them what happened between Tony and me. They both came rushing over to talk to me. We talked for a few hours and ordered some food. They left at about eight o'clock and I decided that I should call Tony and see if he'd calmed down. His line was busy, so I drove over here. I know it sounds stupid, but I thought that the fact that Tony hadn't been honest with me either would give me some bargaining power and maybe we could work things out."

"It's not stupid. It's a logical assumption. So, you drove over here about eight, eight-thirty?"

"I guess so. I didn't have a key so I rang the bell. Tony's car was parked outside so I thought he had to be home. When no one answered the bell, I knocked on the door and it swung open. I walked in and…" Casey stopped talking as her face crumpled and she began to cry softly.

Dana put her arms around her friend and let her cry.

The paramedic suddenly appeared again. "I'm sorry, ladies. We have another call."

Dana stood up and helped Casey to her feet. The paramedic helped them out of the vehicle and Dana led Casey back into the apartment building. Both of their purses were in the hallway on the staircase where they had left them. Dana retrieved her bag and took out some tissues for Casey, who had managed to stop crying again.

Despite the police vehicles, none of the other people in the apartment building had gathered in the hallway.

"Do you know anyone else who lives in this building?" Dana asked Casey.

"The upstairs apartments are being renovated so they are both empty, and the people who live on the first floor are in Europe."

"So no one else is around to have seen or heard anything from Tony's apartment."

"No. I remember being grateful for that this morning when he was yelling and pushing me out of the apartment."

Sam and Bruno were standing just inside the doorway of Tony's apartment watching the forensics team gather evidence.

Bruno turned, saw Dana and Casey, and hurried over to them. He looked at Casey. "Are you doing better now?" he asked in a concerned voice.

"No," Casey said. "But I think I can answer some of your questions now."

Once again, Casey and Dana sat down on the stairs and Sam joined them. Bruno took out his notebook and Casey began her story, but when Bruno asked her what she and

Tony had argued over, she said it was nothing important, just a stupid fight.

"Okay, Casey," Bruno said kindly. "I won't push you now, but eventually you'll have to tell me everything."

"I know," Casey said. "And I will, but I'm so upset now, I can't think straight."

Casey did tell Bruno about Floyd Flannery. When Sam heard the name, his face flushed with anger, but he didn't say anything.

Bruno wrote down the name, but he didn't say anything either, just nodded for Casey to continue her story. She did, skipping ahead to Tony's phone line being busy and deciding to come over to talk to him in person.

"The telephone was on the floor, off the hook," Bruno said.

Casey nodded in agreement. "The door was open and I walked in and saw him on the floor," she said softly.

"Did you touch anything?" Bruno asked.

Casey shook her head vigorously. "No. I knew he was dead so I backed out of the apartment and called Dana."

"Why didn't you call the police?"

"I don't know. The first person I thought to call for help was Dana and she and Sam came right away."

"Okay," Bruno said, closing his notebook. "We'll talk again tomorrow."

"If you're done with Casey," Sam said. "I'll take her and Dana home. Emily called a while ago. Marianne drove her home from the gallery."

"Casey, why don't you stay with me tonight?" Dana offered.

"Thanks, but I think I'd better go to my mother's house. She'll be really upset if I don't get to her before the news of…before the news breaks."

Bruno pulled Dana off to the side. "I'll be here for a while longer and then I have to write up the report. I'll call you in the morning. I've got a lot of questions for you too. How about I ask them over breakfast?"

"Sure," Dana said. "I'll talk to you then."

Sam escorted his two reporters out to his car. It was after eleven when they got to Nina Jordan's house. Sam and Dana wanted to come in and help Casey break the news to her mother, but Casey said she'd rather do it alone, so Sam just walked her to the door and made sure she got inside.

Sam returned to the car and looked at Dana. "Do you think that creep Flannery killed Hunter to get even with Casey?"

"I think it's a possibility, but I hope for Casey's sake it wasn't him. She lost it again when it occurred to her earlier that Tony may have lost his life over one of her investigations."

"I can understand that," Sam said as he pulled away from the curb. "By the way, while Bruno and I were alone, he told me about Hunter's background. I guess your instincts about the guy were right. Did Casey know before she married him?"

"No. I just told her this afternoon."

"She told Bruno they had a fight earlier today and she had left the apartment, but she wouldn't say what the fight was about. Do you know?"

Dana didn't think she should tell Sam about the master plan Casey and her friends had concocted. "I can't discuss it," Dana said. "Casey swore me to secrecy, but it was a fairly bad argument."

"Bruno will probably ask you about it in the morning. Are you going to tell him?"

"Not unless Casey says I can. Besides, I think he'll be more interested in my telling Casey about her new husband's criminal record. This has turned into such a tragedy."

"You know, Bruno is already thinking that Casey may have killed her husband."

Dana turned sharply and looked at her editor. "Did he tell you that?"

"No, but if he thinks a weak kitten like Judy Porter and her baby-faced friend killed her husband, it follows that he'd think the same about Casey, a tough, skilled investigator."

"I have to give Bruno credit for one thing tonight. He saw how torn up Casey was and went easy on her."

"I'll call Troy Kimball first thing in the morning and ask him to speak to Casey. Bruno won't be so kind the next time he questions Casey. She's going to have to tell Bruno everything that happened between her and her husband and Kimball should be with her when she does it."

Dana nodded. Sam was right. Casey was going to be questioned thoroughly about Tony's death and all the details of the master plan would come to light. Dana just hoped Bruno wouldn't see the plan as a motive for murder.

SIXTEEN

DANA'S PHONE STARTED RINGING at 7:00 a.m. when Marianne and Bob called to find out where Casey was and how she was doing. Dana talked to them, giving each as many details as she had while she drank her first cup of coffee.

Sam called to say that he had not been able to reach Troy Kimball but had left a message for him.

Dana showered and dressed in a pair of jeans and a long-sleeved orchid sweater. Her unruly curls had been tamed by a short haircut a few days earlier, so she was able to let them air-dry while she put on enough makeup to make her feel ready to face the world in general and Bruno in particular.

The phone rang again. This time it was Casey.

"How are you doing this morning?" Dana asked.

"Yesterday seems like a nightmare, unreal and impossible."

"What about your mom? How did she take the news?"

"My mom is like the Rock of Gibraltar. She was upset about Tony, but too concerned about me to show it."

"Did you get any sleep?"

"Not much." Casey paused for a long moment. "Dana, do you think I need a lawyer before I talk to Bruno again?"

"It's probably a good idea. Sam has a call in to Troy Kimball. Do you know him?"

"I've seen him in court. He's good."

"So I've heard. He'll be in touch with you." Now Dana paused for a moment. "Listen, Casey, Bruno is going to be here soon. He's going to ask me a lot of questions about what you and I talked about yesterday. How much can I tell him about the master plan?"

"You can tell him the whole humiliating story," Casey said emotionally. "Please. Maybe if he hears it from you first, he won't think so badly of me."

"Bruno is your friend, Casey. He's not going to hold something like that against you."

"He's going to think I killed Tony."

"That's ridiculous." Even as she said it, Dana remembered telling Judy Porter the same thing the day she picked her up from the hospital, but that was exactly what had happened.

Dana's doorbell rang. "He's here now," Dana told Casey. "I'll call you later."

Dana hung up the phone and went to the door.

"Good morning," Bruno said cheerfully. He was holding a grocery bag from Sunflower Market.

"What's in the bag?" Dana asked as she stood on her toes to kiss him lightly on the lips.

"Breakfast."

"You're cooking?"

"Cheese omelets, fruit and biscuits. You can make the coffee."

Bruno handed Dana the grocery bag while he took off his overcoat and scarf. She carried it into the kitchen and set it on the counter. When Bruno joined her a few minutes later, she handed him a steaming mug of black coffee.

"I thought we were going out for breakfast," Dana said as Bruno began taking the ingredients he had purchased out of the bag.

"Not this morning," he said, placing a small platter of fresh fruit on the counter. "You want to set the table in the dining room or should we eat in here?"

"Here is fine," Dana said agreeably.

Dana got two plates, napkins and silverware, and was arranging them on the counter when the telephone rang again.

Dana reached for the phone mounted on the wall next to the counter. "Sorry. People have been calling all morning wanting to know about Casey," she told Bruno. "Hello," she said into the phone.

"The reason I couldn't reach Troy Kimball is because he's at the police station with Judy Porter and Teddy Larson," Sam said without a preamble. "They've both been arrested for the murder of Lucas Porter. Have you talked to Bruno this morning?"

"He's right here in my kitchen."

"Apparently he came to the gallery to arrest the pair last night, but left when you called him away. However, he called the station and sent two uniforms over there to do the honors while he was at the Hunter crime scene. Marianne and Emily had already left, but there were still plenty of other people there to witness the event. They just interviewed Del on the morning news and he is very upset."

"Of course he is. I was afraid Bruno was going to disrupt the showing," Dana said, glaring at her boyfriend, who was busy grating two kinds of cheese for the omelets and pretending not to listen to Dana's end of the conversation.

"I'm going to the office to make sure the story gets the proper coverage. See how much information you can wheedle out of Bruno and call me there."

"I will. Thanks for letting me know," Dana said. She hung up the phone and spoke to Bruno's broad back. "That was Sam."

"Really? How is he this morning?"

"He's okay, but he told me that my dear friend, Del Pit-man, is very upset."

"That's not surprising," Bruno said as he turned on a burner and melted some butter in Dana's Teflon-lined frying pan. Then he deftly whipped cream into the eggs he had broken neatly into a bowl on the counter next to the stove.

Dana got off the stool and walked over to stand next to Bruno. "Why didn't you tell me you had Judy and Teddy arrested last night?"

"Sorry, sweets, I didn't know you wanted me to report to you every time I made an arrest."

"Why did you have them arrested?" Dana asked.

Bruno poured the egg mixture into the hot frying pan and stirred it gently. "I told you on the phone last night. I uncovered some new evidence."

"What evidence?"

"The trick to omelets is turning them at just the right time. My mom taught me that. She's really excited about seeing you again."

"You can be such a jerk," Dana told him.

"See, that's why I thought we should have breakfast here this morning. It's embarrassing when you call me names in a restaurant."

Dana turned and walked out of the kitchen. She intended to leave the apartment and drive to the newspaper office, but the telephone rang before she got to the front closet where her coat was hanging.

"Hello," Dana said, answering the Mickey Mouse phone her nieces and nephews had given her for Christmas.

"Dana, I just remembered something," Casey said in a soft voice.

"What's that?"

"When we were in Las Vegas, Tony got a little freaked

out and insisted that we change hotels. He said that he saw someone he knew from a few years ago and didn't want to talk to the guy. We were at the Excalibur where we got married and Tony moved us off the strip to a hotel in Henderson."

"A few years ago might mean that he saw someone he was in prison with," Dana said.

"Breakfast is ready," Bruno shouted from the kitchen.

"I hear Bruno," Casey said. "Can you ask him if he can find out anything about the time Tony was in prison? Like the possibility that he got into fights with other inmates?"

"I'll talk to him about that and about Tony's brother, who is still in prison."

Dana hung up and hurried into the kitchen. The omelets were on plates on the counter. "Juice or coffee?" Bruno asked.

"Juice," Dana replied, sliding onto one of the two bar-stools at the counter.

Bruno poured her a glass of orange juice and then settled himself on the second stool next to her. "Who was on the phone?" he asked casually.

"Casey. She remembered something that happened in Las Vegas that may have some bearing on Tony's murder."

Bruno groaned. "Let's table the murder talk until after breakfast."

"Okay," Dana replied, cutting into her omelet. The melted cheese oozed onto the plate. She reached for a cres-cent roll and dipped it into the cheese and took a bite. "This is wonderful. You are a much better cook than I am."

"My mama insisted that all of us kids learn how to cook and clean."

"So did my mom, but I always preferred feeding the chickens. My brother Kevin is the cook in the family."

"When we get married, I'll do all the cooking and buy you some pet chickens to feed."

"What about the cleaning?"

"I'll hire a maid."

"Chickens and a maid. I think that's the best offer I've had to date." Dana took another bite of her omelet. "Your mama makes the best spaghetti sauce. Did she teach you how to make that?"

"It's her secret recipe, locked in a vault to be opened only in the event of her death."

"You're kidding."

"Ask her when you see her. Did I tell you she said she's really looking forward to seeing you again?"

"You told me that earlier when I asked what new evidence you uncovered in the Porter case."

Bruno nodded. "Oh yes, that's when you called me a jerk."

Dana finished the last of her omelet and turned on the stool to face Bruno. "I'll give you another chance," she said. "What new evidence?"

"I need an apology first."

"You broke their alibi, didn't you?"

"Maybe."

"Oh, give it up, Bruno," Dana said, sliding off the stool. She began stacking the dirty dishes. "You know you're dying to tell me. You just like to make me beg for details. Well, I'm not going to beg or apologize."

Bruno got off the stool and stood silently while Dana put the plates into her dishwasher. Then he grabbed her and imprisoned her in his arms. "You are the most impossible woman I've ever known," he said. "And I'm too tired to fight with you this morning."

Dana didn't say anything nor did she struggle to free herself from Bruno's embrace. She liked being in his arms for two reasons: it was warm and comforting there and it meant that he was going to tell her what she wanted to know. She leaned her head against his broad chest and waited.

"Sally Larson lied to protect the kids. The guy in the pizza parlor downstairs saw Sally go out at three with her steady boyfriend the afternoon of the murder and she didn't come back until a little after midnight when he was closing up."

"When did the coroner say that Lucas was killed?" Dana asked.

"Between those very same hours," Bruno replied. "But the important thing is that Sally Larson lied about being with Judy and Teddy. And shortly after Sally left the building, Judy and Teddy came out and drove off in Sally's car."

"That's doesn't mean that they killed Lucas," Dana said stubbornly.

"There's something else. The lab guys found a hammer in the weeds near the murder scene. It matches up with the injuries on Porter's head. Teddy Larson works at a hardware store where they sell that very same hammer."

"Circumstantial," Dana said.

Bruno laughed. "You never give up, do you?"

Dana's telephone rang again and Bruno reluctantly let go of her so she could answer it. "Detective Bruno," she said after finding out who was on the phone, "it's for you."

The caller was Bruno's sometime partner, Jack O'Brien. Crescent Hills was still small enough that there were only three homicide detectives on the force. Bruno had been on the force the longest, so he often worked cases on his own. When he needed someone to help with the workload, O'Brien or the youngest member of the force, Donald Blackwell, helped him.

Bruno got on the phone. "I'm off duty and I left my cell and pager in the car," he said in response to Jack's first question. Then he listened for a few minutes and hung up.

"Well, that's interesting," he told Dana. "Tony Hunter's ex-cellmate got out last month and was arrested again early this morning right here in Crescent Hills."

"For what?"

"Got into a fight at a bar downtown."

"How did they know he was Tony's cellmate?"

"He told the arresting officer that he was here to see his old friend, Tony Hunter. Wanted to call Tony and get him to bail him out of jail."

"Casey said there was a guy in Vegas that Tony wanted to avoid. She said he got kind of freaked out and insisted that they move to another hotel off the strip."

"Could be the cellmate," Bruno said.

"You see," Dana said sweetly, "what we have here is a give-and-take arrangement. When we stop fighting and share our information, things between us go much smoother."

Bruno pulled her into his arms again and kissed her. "I love you, kid," he said as he released her. "How about dinner tonight?"

"Where are you going now?" Dana asked.

"To the station to question the cellmate. Then I have to have Casey come in so I can get her to tell me all the details she was withholding last night."

"I know some of those details," Dana said quickly. "In fact she wants me to tell you some of those details. Why don't I ride downtown with you?"

"I'm not letting you near the cellmate and you can't talk to Judy Porter, Teddy Larson, or Casey."

"I'm going to the newspaper office. Sam asked me to come in."

Bruno shrugged. "Okay, let's go."

Dana got her purse, put on her heavy coat and wrapped a scarf around her head.

On the way to the station, Dana told Bruno about the master plan.

"Write down the names of Casey's crazy girlfriends. They all have to be questioned," he said with a huge grin softening his otherwise stern features.

"Why?"

"Just for laughs," Bruno said. "Just for laughs."

SEVENTEEN

INSTEAD OF GOING INTO the newspaper building, when she left the police station Dana braved the cold wind and walked to the art gallery. As she suspected the gallery was closed, but Del's car was in the parking lot.

Dana tapped on the glass window of Del's office. He moved the drape aside, saw her standing there, and rushed to let her inside.

"You look half-frozen," Del said with concern. "Hot tea or coffee?"

"Tea sounds good," Dana told him.

Del settled her into his office and brewed some hot water for tea in the electric kettle he kept behind a fancy screen in his office.

Dana took a few sips of the hot orange spiced tea before she spoke to Del again. "I'm sorry about the scene Bruno caused last night."

"Don't be, darling." Del said with a sly smile. "After the police took Judy and Teddy away, the remaining patrons couldn't wait to buy what was left of Judy's artwork. I sold every painting."

"I see," Dana said slowly. "Sam said they interviewed you on television this morning and you were very upset."

"Well, of course, I'm upset," Del said, trying to suppress a grin. "But apparently, Bruno uncovered some pretty damning evidence or Judy and Teddy would not be in jail right now. Do you know when their hearing is?"

"Tomorrow morning at 10:00 a.m.," Dana replied. "Are you going to be there?"

"I think it's the least I can do. I understand that they have a very competent attorney."

"Yes. Troy Kimball is a good man. Sam has also arranged for him to represent Casey. He's at the station waiting for her now. I wanted to stick around, but Bruno told me I couldn't talk to anyone, so I decided to come over here and see how you were doing. Obviously, I was worried about you for nothing. You're fine."

"Wait a minute," Del said urgently. "What happened to Casey?"

"Her husband was murdered last night."

"I didn't know Casey had a husband."

"She got married in Las Vegas at the beginning of last week. They got back to town on Friday evening and he was murdered last night."

"Is that why you and Sam went rushing out of here?"

"Yes. I thought Marianne or Emily might have told you what happened?"

"No, but then I was so busy I hardly spoke to them. My stars," Del said. "This used to be such a nice quiet town."

"Listen, Del," Dana said, finishing the tea in her cup. "That's the other reason I'm here. I promised to help Judy Porter, but I don't know what I can do now. Teddy's mother lied about being with them the night of the murder and there's some other incriminating evidence that will come out at the hearing tomorrow."

"So you think that Judy and Teddy really killed her husband?"

"I don't know. I just know that I have no leads to follow and now with Casey in trouble…"

Del interrupted her. "Don't tell me Bruno thinks Casey murdered her bridegroom."

"I don't think so. We're supposed to have dinner later and I'm hoping he'll share his views on the case with me, but sometimes Bruno can be very stubborn."

"I understand, darling," Del said calmly. "And I appreciate everything you've already done to help Judy and Teddy. I think it's out of our hands now."

"Yes, I think it is," Dana agreed.

The morning was almost gone and Del was going to leave the gallery, so he gave Dana a ride back to the *Globe* building. She went directly to Sam's office.

"Come in here and read the copy on Hunter's murder," Sam said as soon as he saw her.

Dana sat down with her coat still on and read the copy Sam handed her. Tony Hunter's murder had already been reported in the early-morning edition, but the details had been sparse and there had been no mention that he was recently married to one of the *Globe*'s investigative reporters. In this story it said Hunter was survived by his wife, Cassandra Hunter, and a brother, John.

Dana lowered the page she was reading and looked at Sam. "Do you think the brother has been notified of Tony's death?"

"I don't know. I got his name from the archives of the *Chicago Sun-Times*. They covered the trial. John was sequestered at the Illinois Correctional Facility."

"Was?"

"He was released last week after serving twenty-three years of a twenty-five year sentence."

"Sam," Dana said urgently. "Do you think it's possible that he came here, found out that Tony had spent all the money from the robbery, and killed him?"

"It's possible."

"This morning Casey called me and said she remembered that when they were in Las Vegas, Tony got upset because he saw someone from his past that he didn't want to deal with and insisted that they move to another hotel in a neighboring town."

"Casey didn't see the guy?"

"What guy?" Casey asked.

Dana and Sam looked up, surprised to see Casey and Troy Kimball standing in the doorway to Sam's office.

"Come on in," Sam said quickly. He went out into the newsroom to get another chair and brought it into his office. Then he closed the door so they wouldn't be disturbed.

Casey looked better than she had last night, but her face was pale. "We've just come from talking to Bruno," she said flatly as she settled herself in the chair next to Dana.

Dana reached out and squeezed her hand. "How did it go?"

Troy Kimball answered for her. "Bruno was okay, but then Jack O'Brien came in and he wasn't so nice. He's one of the cops that always operates on the premise that the spouse is the guilty party."

"Jack called my apartment looking for Bruno this morning," Dana told them. "He had just arrested Tony Hunter's ex-cellmate so I guess that got him involved in the case."

"Bruno had me take a look at the guy to see if I recognized him. I didn't, but I guess the guy admitted that he saw Tony and me in Las Vegas, but we disappeared before he got a chance to talk to us," Casey said.

"Is he a suspect?" Sam asked.

"No," Troy replied. "He spent the entire afternoon and evening at a bar downtown. Lots of witnesses, including the guy he got in a fight with, said he didn't leave until the cops came and arrested him."

Sam looked at Troy Kimball. "Since Casey is here, I'm assuming O'Brien couldn't come up with a reason to hold her."

"Right, but I think he's going to keep trying to find one. However, it may all disappear when the results of the autopsy come back. If they determined that Hunter was killed later in the afternoon after Casey left the apartment, we've got witnesses that can testify to her whereabouts."

Casey's eyes filled with tears. "Why would I kill Tony and then go back there again that night?" Sam offered Casey a tissue from the box on his desk. She wiped her eyes as her cell phone began to ring. "It's my mother," Casey said when she read the caller ID display. "Excuse me." She got up and walked away from the group to answer her mother's call.

"I'm going to try and track down Tony Hunter's brother," Dana announced softly. "Sam found out that he was released from prison last week."

"I don't want you going to talk to that guy alone," Sam warned.

"I won't."

"How are you going to find him?" Troy wanted to know.

"My secretary's boyfriend works with the parole boards here and in Chicago. I'm going to ask him to get an address for me."

"Bruno probably has that information already," Sam said.

"I'm sure he does, but I don't think he'll let me come along to interview him."

"Bruno will be tied up most of the day with the Porter case," Kimball said. "He has to testify at the hearing tomorrow and needs to meet with the prosecutor."

Casey came rushing back to the group. "My mom said the police were at her house looking for me."

"When?"

"About twenty minutes ago."

"They'll be here next," Kimball said resignedly.

As if on cue, the door to Sam's office opened and Bruno walked in. "I'm sorry to interrupt," he said, looking directly at Casey. "But I need you to come back to the station for more questioning."

"Are you arresting her?" Troy Kimball asked.

"He'd better not be," Dana said, stepping between Casey and Bruno.

"I'm not arresting her," Bruno said, turning his attention to Dana. "We just have more questions."

Dana stepped aside and she and Sam watched silently as Bruno escorted Casey and her attorney out of the office.

"Call me when you're done," Dana shouted after the group.

Bruno turned around. "I'll pick you up at seven for dinner."

"I'm going to my office to call Marianne," Dana told Sam as soon as Bruno was gone. "Greg was coming back from Chicago today. If I can get an address, I'm going to Chicago to talk to Hunter tonight."

"I'll go with you," Sam said firmly. "That way I won't have to worry about you and I won't be here when Bruno realizes you stood him up tonight."

EIGHTEEN

BY FIVE O'CLOCK, Sam and Dana were on their way to Chicago to see John Hunter. Greg had called the commander at his old precinct. He knew the head of the parole board and even though it was Sunday, Dana was able to get an address for Hunter.

Sam was driving because Dana had driven downtown that morning with Bruno and didn't have a car. As the sun began to set, the air got colder and Dana was glad she was wearing a warm long-sleeved sweater under her coat and had on wool socks with her jeans and tennis shoes. Fortunately, the new snow they had been predicting for the last few days had still not materialized.

Dana's cell phone rang. It was Bruno. "Hi, sweets," he said casually.

"What's going on with Casey?" she answered suspiciously.

Bruno laughed. "If I arrested her, I wouldn't be calling you. She answered my questions. I also talked to her two girlfriends and they all left together, probably to get a drink and talk about how attractive I am."

"How do you know they're not talking about Troy Kimball? He's pretty darn attractive."

"He's also got a big gold wedding ring on his finger. I don't."

"What questions did you have to ask Casey that you couldn't have asked right there in Sam's office?"

"I'm sure she'll give you all the details."

"Right. Listen, Bruno, something has come up and I'm not going to be able to go to dinner with you."

"Why? What are you doing?"

"I'm with Sam. We're checking on a story for the paper."

"What kind of a story?"

"You ask a lot of questions," she said in a light tone. "You should be a cop."

"Very amusing. I've got another call. Ring me when you get done. I still have questions for you."

"Sure. Bye."

Dana clicked off the phone. "Saved by another call. I'm going to call Casey. Bruno said she and her girlfriends left the station together. I assume he questioned them to put together a timeline for Casey's activities yesterday afternoon. The coroner must have fixed the time of death."

"Our coroner is pretty good, but he'd only be able to estimate it within several hours, unless the body was still warm when the lab guys arrived last night."

"Do you think it was?"

"I don't know. I just looked at it from the doorway. Find out what Casey has to say."

Dana dialed Casey's cell phone number, but Casey didn't answer. Then she tried Nina Jordan's phone and Nina told her that Casey had called and said she was going to dinner with Cathy and Carmen. "Have her call me on my cell phone when she gets in, please," Dana said.

They were driving on the highway now and Dana told Sam about her meeting with Del Pitman that morning.

"He sold all of Porter's paintings? Just goes to show what they say is true: there's no such thing as bad publicity. Have you decided to drop the case now?" Sam asked.

"I don't have a choice, Sam. Sally Larson lied about being with Judy and Teddy the night Lucas disappeared. They also found a hammer that they think is the murder weapon and it's an item sold in the hardware store where Teddy works."

"Bruno told you all of that?"

She nodded. "After some prodding, but only because he knows it will be brought out in the hearing tomorrow morning."

"So it looks like these two kids are guilty after all."

"Yes. I'm afraid so," Dana said, although her instincts still told her that they were not capable of such a brutal murder.

They fell silent for a while as they were getting closer to Chicago and traffic had picked up significantly. Sam got off at one of the downtown exits and put Hunter's address into his GPS unit. He waited while the unit brought up a map and directions to Hunter's apartment.

"Turn right on Polk Street and follow it to Forty-seventh Street," the electronic voice on the GPS unit instructed.

"Greg warned me that Hunter lives in a very undesirable neighborhood," Dana told Sam.

"I know. That's one of the reasons I'm driving you there."

"Thanks," she said with a smile.

Twenty minutes later, Sam parked the car in front of a rundown three-story building. They got out of the car and went into the hallway. There were mailboxes on the wall in the cramped space, but most of them didn't have doors, and there were no doorbells.

"Hunter lives in number 302," Dana said.

"Let's take the stairs," Sam joked. "I don't want to waste time waiting for the elevator."

The stairs were worn and wooden and filled with various types of debris. Dana and Sam trudged up them ignoring the noises and smells that assaulted them as they climbed the steps.

On the second floor, there were children playing on the

landing. Three small boys were crashing trucks and cars into the walls.

"Hi," Dana said as she passed by them.

"Who are you?" one of the boys who appeared to be about five years old asked.

She stopped. "I'm a friend of Mr. Hunter's. Do you know him?"

"Nope," the little boy said. "I don't know nobody with that name, but another man just asked me the same thing."

"Sounds like Hunter may have company," Sam said. "Is the other man still up there?"

The boy shrugged and looked at his two playmates. They were busy with their trucks and didn't seem interested in their friend or Dana and Sam.

Dana and Sam climbed two more flights to the third floor. The apartment numbers were painted on the brown doors in yellow fluorescent paint. Number 302 was the second apartment to the left of the staircase.

As they approached the door, a gunshot rang out from inside the apartment and something big and heavy fell to the floor.

Sam banged on the door. His knock was answered by another gunshot that splintered the thin wood on the door.

"Call 911," Sam whispered as he and Dana braced themselves against the wall of the apartment and moved down the hallway away from it.

Dana heard the sound of breaking glass inside the apartment as the dispatcher answered her 911 call. She quickly reported that shots had been fired and gave the address of the building.

Suddenly other doors on the third floor opened. Sam shouted at them to stay inside their apartments.

"I'll bet the shooter went out the window to the fire escape," Sam said. "I'll try and catch him."

Sam started for the staircase, but Dana grabbed the sleeve of his overcoat and hung on. "Don't be crazy," she yelled. "He's got a gun, you don't."

The other doors opened again, and this time people came into the hallway. "What's going on?" a big man with tattoos on his arms yelled as he approached them.

"Someone shot at us from inside this apartment," Sam told him.

Without a moment's hesitation, the big man slammed into the door of 302 and sent it banging against the inside wall of the room. He ran inside with Sam and Dana right behind him.

A man who looked a lot like Tony Hunter was on the floor bleeding. Sam and Dana stopped in their tracks, but the neighbor ran over and knelt down next to the man.

"Oh, no," he cried. "Someone shot Johnny. Call the police. Call an ambulance."

"We already did," Sam told him. "They're on their way."

Dana looked at the shattered window and the metal bar stool that was on its side on the fire escape. It didn't take much thought to surmise that the shooter had broken the window in order to flee down the fire escape.

More neighbors were in the hallway crowding the doorway to get a look inside the apartment. The big man stood up and shook his head. "Too late, baby," he said. "He's dead."

As sirens sounded in the distance, Dana remembered the boys on the second floor landing. She hurried out of the apartment and down the stairs.

The little boys were gone, probably scared inside by the gunshots and the shouting. Dana began knocking on doors. Finally the last one at the end of the hallway opened and the little boy she had talked to earlier answered it.

"Hi," Dana said. "Is your mom at home?"

"She's sleeping."

"Where are your friends?"

"They're not my friends, they're my brothers," he said. "They got scared and ran in the closet."

"That was smart of them," she said. "I was wondering if you could tell me about the man you saw going upstairs just before my friend and I saw you."

"He was old and had a black hat with a red bird on it."

"How old do you think he was?"

The boy shrugged. "I don't know."

"Did you see his hair?"

"I told you he was wearing a hat," the little boy said as if she were a dunce.

"So you did," Dana replied. "Can you tell me more about the hat?"

"No," he said just before he slammed the door in her face.

Dana was about to knock again when two uniformed policemen came running up the stairs.

"You the lady that called?" one of them asked her.

"Yes. It's the third floor, apartment 302," she replied.

"Okay. Come with us, please."

Dana followed the officers up the stairs. By now, Sam had managed to get the other neighbors away from the door and grouped together at the far end of the hall. The big man who was obviously a friend of Hunter's was still in the apartment kneeling by the body.

Dana heard more feet clamoring up the stairs and within a few minutes two paramedics appeared dragging a gurney.

One of the policemen who had entered the apartment came out and told the paramedics to leave, confirming the neighbor's earlier announcement. John Hunter was dead.

The arrival of the police had caused all the neighbors

except for Hunter's big friend to scurry back to their apartments and lock their doors.

Dana and Sam stood in the hallway with him while the police assessed the situation and called in their report.

"I take it you were a friend of Hunter's?" Dana asked the man.

"We were in the joint together. I got him this apartment when he got out last week. Who are you?"

"My name is Dana Sloan and the gray-haired gentleman talking to the police is Sam McGowan. We work for a newspaper in Crescent Hills."

"What did you want with Johnny?"

"I knew his brother, Tony. I came here to tell him that Tony was murdered last night."

"His brother was killed?" the big man said incredulously. "What the hell is going on?"

"I don't know. Did Johnny tell you anything about his brother?"

"Just that he was mad at him about something and was going to see him as soon as he got permission from his parole officer."

"Dana? What are you doing here?"

Dana turned around to see Jack O'Brien standing on the landing behind her. Jack had reddish blond hair and a ruddy complexion. He was as tall as Bruno, but lean and lanky-looking.

"Hi, Jack," Dana said. "What are you doing here?"

"I asked you first," Jack said without any humor in his voice.

"Sam and I came here to talk to John Hunter. Unfortunately, we arrived too late. Someone shot him."

Jack swore softly under his breath. "He's dead?"

"Yes," Dana replied.

"Bruno sent me here to give him the bad news about his

brother and ask him some questions." Jack looked curiously at Dana. "Bruno know you're here?"

"No, he doesn't."

Jack nodded and pulled a cell phone out of his pocket and dialed a number. "Hey, buddy. I'm here at Hunter's apartment in Chicago and guess what? Someone shot the guy." He listened for a few seconds, then continued, "Yeah. Damn shame isn't it? But listen, guess who I found standing in the hallway outside Hunter's apartment, your pretty little girlfriend." Jack smiled as he listened to whatever Bruno was saying, then held out the phone to Dana. "He wants to talk to you.'

Dana stared at the phone for a few seconds then finally took it from Jack. "Hello," she said casually as if she had run into Jack at the shopping mall, rather than a murder scene.

"What are you doing there?" Bruno asked in a menacing tone.

"Sam and I came here to talk to Hunter, but someone got here before us. He's dead."

"Are you and Sam okay?"

"Yes."

"Good, now get yourselves back to Crescent Hills. I want to talk to both of you."

"I don't think we'll be allowed to leave real soon," Dana told him.

"Why not?"

"We're witnesses."

"Oh, great," Bruno said loudly. "You saw the shooter?"

"Not exactly. When we got to Hunter's door we heard a shot. Sam pounded on the door and the shooter fired the gun at us. Then he threw a metal bar stool through the window and ran down the fire escape."

"You just can't stay out of trouble, can you?" Those

were the words Bruno used when he was about to lecture her on her job and the dangers of it.

Dana was in no mood to hear it again. "I've got to go. The police want to question me." Dana pushed the button that ended the call. She handed the phone back to Jack O'Brien.

"I'll bet he's steamed, huh?" Jack asked.

"Of course not," Dana said. "Bruno understands that I'm just doing my job and he supports me."

"You wish," Jack replied with a big smile. "Well, I guess I'll go and introduce myself to the local cops." He walked into the apartment with his detective shield held out in front of him.

Dana turned around to find that Hunter's prison mate had vanished, but Sam was standing in the hallway now. "Bad luck to have O'Brien show up," Sam said.

Dana nodded. "Bruno is fuming."

"He'll get over it," Sam assured her.

"I told him we were witnesses and we'd probably be here awhile."

"Right. The uniforms reported in. The homicide detectives should be showing up any minute."

"I'm starving. I haven't eaten since breakfast this morning," Dana said absently.

"Maybe they'll have doughnuts at the police station," Sam told her.

Dana nodded. "What happened to the big guy?"

"When no one was looking he went back to his apartment, got a jacket and hat and left the building."

"He's not really a witness," Dana said. "But he did tell me that he and Hunter were in prison together and he got him this apartment."

"Interesting."

"He also said that John was angry with Tony for some

reason and wanted to go to Crescent Hills to see him, but was waiting for permission from his parole officer."

"Very interesting," Sam said.

NINETEEN

IT WAS WELL AFTER midnight when Sam dropped Dana off at her apartment. They had been interrogated separately by a pair of Chicago homicide detectives and signed statements for them.

Dana told them about the little boys on the second floor who claimed to see the man who was in Hunter's apartment when she and Sam arrived. One of the detectives promised they would check it out.

There were no doughnuts at the Chicago station and the coffee they brought Dana was so strong she feared drinking it would keep her awake for a week.

Before they left the station, Sam called the newsroom at the *Globe* and dictated a story about John Hunter's murder in Chicago.

On the way home, Sam made a stop at a fast-food place and they ate their dinner in the car.

Dana was exhausted. She had turned off her cell phone at the police station and had not bothered to turn it on again. Whatever messages were on it could wait until morning. She also decided not to check her messages on her home line either. Both phones probably contained messages from Bruno and she was not up to arguing with him tonight.

"If Bruno's car is in my lot," she had told Sam when they arrived at her building, "don't stop. Just take me to the nearest hotel."

Sam laughed. "You've got to talk to him sometime."

"I'll see him tomorrow in court. That will be soon enough to face his wrath."

"You can say it was all my idea," Sam offered.

Dana brightened. "I just might do that."

Dana's head was swirling from all the questions the police had thrown at her. She was grateful that Jack O'Brien had decided to return to Crescent Hills and had not insisted on being present when she and Sam were giving their statements.

Dana didn't like Jack much, maybe because he obviously disapproved of her relationship with Bruno. Jack was one of those cops who thought reporters were people who only got in the way and made his job more difficult. Dana thought that Jack got in the way of his own investigations because he made snap judgments about people and situations that often took him off in the wrong direction.

In her bedroom, Dana stripped off her clothes and decided to take a long hot shower. She was uptight from the unsettling events of the night and felt grimy from her time in the run-down apartment building and the noisy chaos of the Chicago police station in the same neighborhood.

The shower helped and Dana fell asleep immediately. However, her dreams contained images of little boys, red birds and John Hunter's dead body. She was relieved when her alarm clock roused her from sleep the next morning.

After completing her morning rituals that included two cups of freshly brewed coffee, Dana braced herself and listened to the messages on her cell phone.

The first one was from Casey. "Hi, Dana. Bruno had more questions for me, but he seemed satisfied with my answers. He also questioned Carmen and Cathy, who verified the time they spent with me. I guess the coroner's report came in, but Bruno wouldn't tell us what it said. He did say that my fingerprints were on the golf club on the living room floor. I told him Tony and I often shared the same putter when we practiced. I'm really grateful to have Troy Kimball at my side. He is a very good lawyer and that may be why Bruno went easy on me again today. I'm coming to the office tomorrow. I need to work and stay busy."

Dana erased the message. She hadn't expected Casey to come into the office for several days, but she understood her need to stay busy and focus on something other than the unspeakable violence that had ended her marriage to Tony Hunter.

Dana wondered if Casey had heard about Tony's brother being murdered in a similar manner. *The two murders are very similar.* Although she had been at both crime scenes that thought had not really registered in her brain last night. She had told the Chicago detectives about Tony's murder occurring the night before, but they didn't seem to care about a murder that happened fifty miles away in Crescent Hills. She could understand that. Chicago was gigantic compared to Crescent Hills, and the neighborhood where Hunter was murdered was probably a haven for criminals and crime.

Dana thought back to the pandemonium at the Chicago police station. It made the Crescent Hills station seem like a haven of peace and tranquility.

The next three messages on her cell phone dispelled all thoughts of peace and tranquility. They were from Bruno asking her to call him no matter what time she got home. The irritation in his voice came through loud and clear, and since she had not called him when she got home, he would be even more irritated today.

Maybe Jack O'Brien was right about her relationship with Bruno. They always seemed to be at odds with each other over their respective jobs. It was a miracle that they had stayed together this long. Dana often admitted that she and Bruno were an unlikely couple. They had walked away from each other more than once, but had always found a way to work through their problems and come together again. Dana shook her head as if to avoid any more thoughts of Detective Al Bruno and the bumpy road of love they had chosen to travel.

The last message was from Marianne, wanting to know if she had found Hunter's address okay.

Dana dropped the cell phone into her purse and checked the messages on her home phone. Three more identical messages from Bruno that she quickly erased, and one from her mother.

"Hi, sweetheart," her mom's voice called out. "I know you're busy. Just wanted to let you know I'm thinking of you. Call when you can."

Dana saved that message. Her mom's cheerful tones always made her feel better and she often listened to her messages several times. After seeing Bruno that morning in court, Dana would probably have to listen to her mom's message several more times.

Dressed in a soft gray pantsuit with a plain white blouse underneath the jacket, Dana pulled on her coat. It was still across the back of the sofa with her scarf. She had been too tired to hang it up when she came in the night before.

The drive to the office only took fifteen minutes that morning. She was a little later than usual and traffic was lighter. She parked in her designated space in the *Globe* lot and hurried into the building.

Marianne and Casey were both in the reception area when Dana came through the door. Marianne was behind her desk and Casey was sitting in one of the visitor chairs.

As usual, Marianne looked gorgeous in a kelly green sweater with matching pants. Casey on the other hand reverted back to the way she looked before the master plan. Her hair was pulled back and fastened with a rubber band. She wore no makeup and was dressed in a pair of jeans and a sweatshirt.

Dana pulled the scarf from her head and shook her curls free of the static from the scarf. She had gone to bed with her hair damp from the shower last night and had to use lots of hairspray to subdue her curls this morning.

"We just heard about John Hunter," Marianne said.

"I can't believe this," Casey said woodenly. "First Tony, now his brother. The murders have to be connected."

"That's just what I was thinking this morning," Dana replied.

"What do the police think?" Marianne asked.

"The Chicago Police didn't seem too interested in the fact that Tony was killed within twenty-four hours of his brother. It's a big, busy precinct, but I'm going to ask Bruno to communicate with them. That is, if Bruno is speaking to me this morning."

"Oh, he's speaking all right," Marianne said. "He's called twice already. Wants you to call him back as soon as you get in."

"How does he sound?" Dana asked.

"Like a lamb."

Dana laughed. "I'm sure you're just saying that so I'll call him and he'll stop bugging you. Okay. I'll do it." She turned to Casey. "As soon as Bob comes in, we need to have a meeting. It'll be short because I want to go to the courthouse and sit in on Judy Porter's hearing."

Dana went into her office, hung up her coat and scarf on the wooden coat tree in the corner and went to her desk and dialed Bruno's direct line at the station.

"Detective Bruno," he said, answering on the first ring.

"Hi," Dana said. "Sorry I didn't get back to you last night, but it was really late when we got back from Chicago."

"I was up," he said pointedly.

"I was too exhausted to argue with you, Bruno."

"Who said I wanted to argue? I just wanted to make sure you were all right."

"Physically, I'm fine. Mentally, I'm a little stressed."

"I talked to Jack this morning. He wasn't much help. I'd like to get your version of the facts. Can we have lunch today?"

"If you'd like."

"I'd like to take you off on a Caribbean cruise and forget all the murder and mayhem here, but lunch will have to do."

"I'll be at the hearing. I'll catch up with you there."

"I'm wearing the brown suit, the one that makes women fall at my feet. Can you take it?"

"I'll brace myself," Dana said with a smile in her voice. "See you later."

Dana hung up the phone as Bob and Casey came into the office.

"How's the love of your life today?" Bob asked with an impish grin. "I heard Jack O'Brien ratted you out last night."

"Who told you that?" Dana asked.

"Jack O'Brien. He was in the coffee shop downstairs and couldn't wait to report that he ran into you at a murder scene and reported it to Bruno."

"Did he tell you it was Tony's brother that was murdered?" Casey asked.

"I read it in our morning edition." Bob looked at Casey with concern. "Why are you here this morning?"

"I need to keep busy," she said firmly.

"Send her to talk to the lady with the aliens in her

basement," Bob told Dana. "She called me on my cell phone yesterday."

"How did she get your cell phone number?" Dana asked.

"She said the aliens gave it to her. She also said the aliens think I'm overweight and should go on a diet. Come to think of it, the woman's voice sounded a lot like my wife's."

Casey smiled, probably the first time she had done so since she went grocery shopping with Tony on Saturday morning.

"Well, I'm glad you want to stay busy, Casey," Dana said. "I've got a stack of requests here. I haven't had time to go through them but Marianne put the most urgent ones on top."

The intercom buzzed. "Dana," Marianne said. "Floyd Flannery's attorney is on line one insisting that he speak to you."

Casey and Bob were on their feet going through the stack of requests on Dana's desk. Both stopped and stared at the telephone.

Dana shrugged and accessed line one. "Dana Sloan."

"Good morning. I'm wondering if you are aware that my client has been arrested again."

"No. I didn't know that."

"His arrest is based on information given to the police by one of your employees, Cassandra Hunter."

The use of Casey's married name threw Dana a bit, but she quickly recovered. "I know that Mr. Flannery showed up at my employee's apartment on Saturday afternoon and harassed her. That same day her husband was murdered, and given your client's volatile nature, I'm happy to hear that he's in custody again."

"I see. Floyd swore to me that he was nowhere near Mrs. Hunter. Obviously he lied to me again."

"When exactly was he arrested?" Dana asked.

"Yesterday afternoon about five o'clock."

"And he's been in custody ever since?"

"Yes."

"In view of what happened in Chicago last night, that's fortunate for your client."

"I read about the other murder in this morning's paper. You're right. If Floyd was in jail, they can't try and pin that one on him too."

"Exactly."

"Once again, I apologize for talking to you under such unpleasant circumstances. I'm wondering if you'd be free for dinner some evening."

"I'm probably going to testify against your client in court," Dana told him. "Wouldn't that be a conflict of interest?"

"Not if I drop Flannery's case," he answered.

"I'm sorry, I can't," Dana said. "My circumstances won't allow it."

"Well, if your circumstances change, please let me know. I'd drop Floyd like a hot poker."

The phone call ended and Bob was grinning. "He asked you out, didn't he?" Bob asked.

"Yes," Dana admitted.

"I guess he's not acquainted with Detective Al Bruno."

"I guess Bruno may have considered Flannery a suspect in Tony's murder," Casey said haltingly.

"Bruno usually covers all the bases," Dana replied. She glanced at her watch. "Speaking of Detective Bruno, I want to go to Judy Porter's hearing and then I'm having lunch with Bruno. Have you two found enough to keep you busy for the next few days?"

"Most of these cases we can work together," Bob said. "If it's okay with Casey. How about it, kid?"

Casey smiled for the second time that morning. "I think that's a good idea. What do you think, Dana?"

"I agree. I think working is good therapy for you, and having Bob working with you is even better therapy. Just keep me posted on your progress."

TWENTY

THE COURTHOUSE WAS A few blocks from the police station and the *Globe*. Dana decided to walk it because parking at the courthouse was often limited. Besides, the sun was shining and it wasn't nearly as cold as it had been the day before.

Dana passed through security and found the courtroom where the Porter hearing was being held.

"Hey, Dana," one of the reporters from the paper assigned to cover the courthouse called out as she sailed past her. She was new on the staff and Dana didn't remember what her name was, but she smiled and waved at her.

There were not many people in the room, but Dana saw Sally Larson sitting by herself looking miserable. She considered going over and talking to the woman, but decided against it. Bruno would see her and think she was throwing her support to the opposing side.

Dana still didn't believe that Judy and Teddy had killed Lucas, so technically she was not on Bruno's side. However, Dana didn't know how she could help them now. Sally's lie meant to protect her son and her friend had backfired, making the pair look all the more guilty.

"Hello, my friend," Del said quietly as he slid onto the empty bench next to Dana.

Dana smiled at him. "I'm glad you're here and I'm sure Judy will appreciate your support."

Troy Kimball entered the courtroom. He was wearing a blue suit that matched his eyes and he looked very handsome.

A few minutes later, Del touched Dana's arm. "Here comes your boyfriend. I assume he's going to present the damaging evidence."

"Yes, I'm afraid so," Dana agreed.

Bruno was wearing his brown suit and it looked great on his large frame. The pale beige shirt and beige and brown tie Dana had given him for Christmas went beautifully with the suit. Dana glanced around the room. The young reporter from the *Globe* did look like she might swoon.

The bailiffs escorted Judy Porter and Teddy Larson into the room and seated them together at the defense table with their lawyer. Kimball leaned over and spoke to them quietly. The two kids looked scared to death and Kimball's words didn't seem to make them feel better.

The prosecutor, a seasoned veteran named Louis Hildago, came in and snapped open his briefcase on his table and started removing papers. Hildago had a reputation for being tough but fair. He and Bruno were friends who sometimes went to ball games together. They were both White Sox fans.

"All rise," the bailiff announced. Everyone stood as the judge entered and took his seat behind the bench.

The proceedings began with the prosecution calling Glenn Harrison to the stand first. He told how he had taken the missing persons report from Judy Porter and noticed that she had bruises that indicated to him that Lucas Porter had abused her.

"Tell me, Detective Harrison, does it make sense to you that Mrs. Porter would report her husband missing when she already knew he was dead?"

Kimball objected and Hildago rephrased the question. However, the answer was the same, a missing persons report was often filed by a spouse who later turned out to be a murderer.

The medical examiner testified that Lucas Porter had been struck in the head repeatedly with a blunt instrument. It had been determined that the instrument was a hammer found in the weeds near the bridge where the victim's body had been tossed in the river.

Bruno took the stand and said that the murder weapon was a hammer sold in the hardware store where Teddy Larson worked.

Kimball got Bruno to admit that there was no bill of sale to prove that Teddy had purchased that particular hammer.

Hildago asked Bruno about the alibi Sally Larson had provided and Bruno told how he had discovered that she was lying to protect her son and Judy Porter.

Dana was surprised when Kimball didn't cross-examine Bruno or call Teddy or Judy to testify. The hearing ended with the judge stating that there was sufficient evidence to send to the grand jury.

Kimball then requested that there be an immediate bail hearing. The judge granted his request and bail for Judy and Teddy was set at $200,000 each, which was quite low in a murder case.

Dana was quite impressed with the way Troy Kimball had argued on behalf of his clients, citing the fact that neither of them had ever been in trouble before and they were not a flight risk.

"At least they won't have to stay in jail any longer," Del said. "I've already made arrangements with the bondsman."

"That's so nice of you, Del," Dana said.

"Judy needs to be free to work on her paintings. I have a waiting list of people who want to buy them now and she's going to need the cash to pay her attorney fees."

Dana looked at her friend and smiled. While many

people would think that Del was putting up the bond to pressure Judy into producing more paintings to line his own pockets, Dana knew better. Del was a good person, a generous person, and he was right in thinking that Judy was going to need as much income as possible to pay her attorney fees.

Dana walked out of the courtroom and stood in the hallway to wait for Bruno, who had stopped to talk to Hildago.

"Hello, Dana," a familiar voice said in her ear.

She turned to see Ben Hughes standing next to her.

"Hello," Dana replied.

"Thanks for talking to me earlier. I appreciate the information."

"I didn't tell you anything you didn't already know," she said.

"You're right. It was actually just an excuse to talk to you and ask you out, but it didn't work out too well for me."

"Are you ready for lunch, sweets?" Bruno had walked up to join them without Hughes noticing. He jumped at the sound of Bruno's voice.

Dana tried to make an introduction, but Ben waved her off. "Detective Bruno and I have already met, several times. Nice seeing both of you again. Have a pleasant lunch."

Hughes walked away and Bruno looked at Dana. "What was he up to?"

"He's Floyd Flannery's attorney."

"I know it, and he shouldn't be talking to you."

"He knows that, but he said he'd drop Flannery like a hot poker if I agreed to go out with him."

Bruno's dark eyes grew a shade darker. "Lucky for Flannery he's going to stick with him."

"Yes, Bruno. And even if he doesn't, I still wouldn't date him. He's not my type."

"What is your type?"

"Big, broad detectives in brown suits."

"Good answer." Bruno smiled and took her arm. "Let's go to Lou's and find a quiet booth. I have a lot of questions for you and some of them are very personal."

Dana sighed. The irritation Bruno had expressed the night before had seemed to vanish with the light of day. Dana wanted to accept the fact that she and Bruno had successfully sidestepped another obstacle in the road, but they still had to get through lunch. As they made their way down the courthouse steps Dana wondered for the thousandth time if the ongoing challenge of these twists and turns in their relationship was what actually kept them together.

Big Lou's Café was next door to the newspaper building and was owned by a lovely lady named Lucille. Her husband was a retired police officer and the restaurant was frequented by a lot of people who worked out of the police station and conducted business at the courthouse.

"Hey, Bruno," Lou called out from behind the cashier's counter. "I saved you that booth in the corner."

"Thanks, Lou. I owe you one," Bruno called back as he and Dana hurried back to a V-shaped booth nestled into a corner of the café between two windows.

"How did you manage this in the middle of the lunch rush?" Dana asked as she slid into the booth and started unbuttoning her coat.

"Bribery."

"Who's getting bribed? You or Lou?"

"Lou, of course. I had to buy two tickets to some charity dinner at the Ventana next week. Actually, I bought three tickets. I thought you and I could take my mama along."

The Ventana was a fairly new resort that had opened

in Crescent Hills the previous summer. It was drawing a number of tourists and conventions to the city.

"That must have been a very hefty bribe."

"It's for the children's wing of the hospital so I thought it was worth the money."

Lou herself came over to the table with two glasses of water and two cups of coffee. She smiled at Bruno. "You look exceptionally handsome today."

"It's the brown suit," Dana told her. "We had to pass out smelling salts to all the women at the courthouse."

"Hi, Dana," Lou said. "Where have you been hiding lately?"

"In my office, behind stacks of files."

"I heard about Casey. What a shocker. How's she doing?"

"She came back to work this morning. She said she wanted to keep busy, but I'm having her work with Bob so he can look out for her."

"You're a smart cookie," Lou said. "Bruno, when are you going to wake up and marry this girl?"

"She's the one who's dragging her feet," Bruno told her.

"Hmmm. Maybe she's even smarter than I thought." Lou softened the remark by giving Bruno a pat on his head like he was one of her sons. "Are you ready to order?"

Bruno ordered a club sandwich with French fries and Dana ordered a cup of chicken noodle soup and half a ham-and-cheese sandwich. Lou made a fresh pot of soup every morning and the sandwiches she served were gigantic, so half was more than enough for Dana.

Lou went off to transfer their order to the kitchen and Bruno decided to get down to business. "Whose idea was it to stand me up and drive to Chicago last night?"

"Would you believe it was Sam's idea?" Dana said with mock sincerity.

"No. Sam probably just went along to keep you out of harm's way."

"Okay. Next question."

"I won't ask how you got Hunter's address. You always seem to find out what you want when you want it. So, you got Hunter's address and went to his apartment building, then what happened?"

Dana told Bruno the whole story including the part about the little boys on the second-floor landing and how she went back and talked to the child after Hunter was murdered and the shooter escaped out the window.

"He shot at you and Sam through the door?"

"Yes."

"And that didn't scare you?" Bruno asked sternly.

"Of course it scared me. Luckily we weren't standing in front of the door. The bullet went straight through it and lodged in the banister. That's when the big guy came out of his apartment to see what was going on."

"The big guy's name is Henry Lindbloom. The Chicago cops are going to pick him up for questioning."

"I don't think he knows anything that can help," Dana said. "He was just as shocked as we were at the shooting."

"We're waiting for Chicago to fax a report on the bullet that killed John Hunter. I want to see if it came from the same gun that killed Tony."

"If so, Casey will no longer be a suspect?"

"She's not one now, at least not as far as I'm concerned. I talked to her girlfriends last night and they swear she was with them until after 8:00 p.m. and the M.E. says Hunter was killed earlier than that."

Dana nodded. "Besides that, the little boys saw a man go up to Hunter's apartment last night, not a woman."

"A man with a red bird on his hat? It was in the report Chicago faxed to me."

"Right."

"Not much to go on. I assume the Chicago guys will go back and question the kids again and other people in the building to see if they saw anything."

"I doubt if there are other witnesses," Dana said. "The hallways were pretty deserted, but someone could have been looking out the windows and saw the shooter running away. Or someone on the street may have seen him."

"The problem is that people in that neighborhood don't like to step forward with information for the police," Bruno replied.

One of the other waitresses came over and delivered their food and their conversation stopped while they both enjoyed the first few bites of their respective lunches.

"The two murders are obviously connected," Dana said after she had finished her soup.

"Obviously."

"It must have something to do with the bank robbery or the time they spent in prison. Henry Lindbloom said that John hadn't seen Tony yet."

"That doesn't mean that they hadn't been communicating."

"True. Casey didn't know anything about Tony's past until I told her on Saturday. Tony claimed he didn't have any family. However, he had golfing buddies and other friends at the country club; maybe he confided in one of them."

"Maybe. It's worth checking out." Bruno reached across the table and grabbed her hand. "When I say it's worth checking out, I mean that as the lead detective on the case, I'm going to check it out."

"Of course," Dana agreed.

"You're going to stay out of it."

Dana removed her hand from his grasp and changed the

subject. "What's going on with Floyd Flannery? Are you going to release him again?"

"He's going to stay in jail until his assault trial. By showing up at Casey's apartment on Saturday, he violated the restraining order the *Globe* filed forbidding him to come near the newspaper office or anyone on your staff."

"I see, and the fact that he was in custody last night rules him out as a suspect in the Chicago murder."

"You didn't answer my question," Bruno said. "You are going to stay out of the Hunter murder cases, aren't you?"

Dana took the last bite of her sandwich and pushed her plate away. Bruno had already finished his lunch and the waitress came over and refilled his coffee cup. Dana passed on the refill and the girl went away again.

Finally, Dana spoke to Bruno again. "We'd have less conflicts in our relationship if you'd stop asking me questions like that. I'm a reporter and a trained investigator and I have a personal interest in the Hunter cases. And I'm not going to lie and say I'm leaving it alone."

"Do you want to have children when we get married?"

"What?"

"Just thought I'd ask a different question."

"We've already discussed the question of children and you know what we decided."

"Yeah, so as the future mother of my children do you understand why I'm concerned about you investigating murders?"

"Oh, my phone is ringing," Dana said, pulling the silent cell phone out of her purse and answering it.

Bruno wasn't fooled. He picked up the lunch check and carried it up to the cashier's counter to pay. Dana stood up, put her coat and scarf on and hurried out of the café.

Bruno caught up with her as she got into the revolving

door at the *Globe* building. He squeezed into the section of the door Dana had entered.

"Who was on the phone?" he asked, putting his arm around her waist.

"I have to get back to my office," she told him. "And you probably have to check in at the station."

"Right. I'll call you later." Bruno bent down and kissed her on the cheek. "Remember the bambinos," he whispered in her ear.

Dana watched him leave the building and stand at the stoplight waiting to cross the street to the station. Then, she pulled off her scarf and unbuttoned her coat as she hurried toward the elevator that would take her up to her office.

TWENTY-ONE

MARIANNE WAS ON THE PHONE when Dana came through the door. "Hold on," she said. "She just walked in." Marianne put the caller on hold. "It's Bruno for you," she told Dana.

"Bruno? I just left him in the lobby." Marianne shrugged. Dana went into her office and pushed the button on the blinking line. "What is it?" she said into the phone.

"I just wanted to know if you missed me."

"You just wanted to know if I was really going to my office," Dana said. "Well, I'm here. Satisfied?"

"For the moment. I'll call you later."

"Good-bye, Bruno," Dana said and dropped the phone back into its cradle before he could respond.

Dana hung up her coat and scarf thinking how much she missed summer when she didn't have to bundle up to go outside and unbundle when she was inside. It wasted so much time.

Marianne came in carrying a few phone messages. "Nothing urgent," she said. "And now that you're back I'm going out to lunch. Do you want me to transfer the phones to the answering service?"

"Please," Dana replied. "Have you heard from Casey or Bob?"

"No. How did the hearing go?"

"As expected, but Kimball got the judge to set bail and Del put up their bonds."

"That was nice of him."

"He's a nice man. I'm going to do some computer research so close my door when you leave."

"Okay. I'll see you in an hour or so."

Dana told Marianne to have a nice lunch and then scooted herself closer to the computer keyboard on her desk. She accessed the Internet, brought up the *Chicago Sun-Times* Web site and logged into her account.

Dana searched the archives using the keywords "Anthony Hunter" and found 106 references. She began scanning the lead-ins to the articles and opened the one that said Hostage Taken In Bank Robbery. When the article appeared on the screen, Dana printed it out.

The next article Dana printed was the one that reported the discovery of the body of the female hostage in an alley several blocks from the bank where she'd been abducted. The woman's name was Sarah Turner and she was twenty-two years old.

Suspects Arrested In Robbery/Murder reported how two brothers, John and Anthony Hunter, had been arrested at the home of John's girlfriend, Mary Lou Bandini. No address was given for Bandini. The article went on to say the arrest had resulted from an anonymous tip. The suspects had appeared in a lineup and the bank teller and other employees had positively identified the Hunter brothers as the bank robbers.

The articles in the archives traced the history of the trial, conviction and sentencing, and Dana printed out all the articles that she needed and put them in chronological order.

By the time Marianne came back from lunch, Dana had made another copy of all the articles and placed them in another file. She handed the file to Marianne and asked her to label it and put it in a safe place.

"What do you want me to label it?" her secretary asked.

"Hunter Crime File," Dana responded.

"I read the story Sam ran about Tony Hunter's brother being murdered last night. It's so bizarre. I didn't mention it this morning because I didn't want to get Casey upset."

"I don't think Casey can be any more upset than she already is," Dana told her. "Maybe finding out how and why this happened will help her."

"What can I do to help?" Marianne asked.

Dana handed Marianne a slip of paper with the name Mary Lou Bandini written on it. "See if you can run a trace on this name. I want to know where she is now. She'd be in her late thirties or early forties."

Globe Investigations subscribed to several databases that could be used to get information on individuals, and Marianne was a whiz at doing research. She flipped her hand through her red tresses and sat down at her desk.

Dana went back to her office and called a friend of hers at the county recorder's office in Cook County, Illinois.

"Hi, Dana," Billy said when he picked up the phone.

Dana and Billy had gone to college together and Billy had married Dana's best friend, Trudy. Dana had been the maid of honor at their wedding.

"How's Trudy and the baby?" Dana asked.

"Both getting fat and sassy," Billy joked. "How are you and the brute getting along these days?"

Dana laughed. "The same as always."

"Bring him to dinner next weekend. We haven't seen you guys in a while."

"We can't come next weekend," Dana said. "Bruno's mother is coming here for a visit."

"Is that good or bad?"

"I'm not sure," Dana said honestly. "Listen, pal, I need a favor."

"Don't you always when you call me at work."

Dana laughed again. "Yes."

"What do you need?"

"I'm investigating two brothers named Hunter who committed a robbery and murder twenty-three years ago. They lived in Chicago, so I'm hoping they were born there in Cook County and you can get me some information off their birth certificates."

"Do you have birth dates?"

"I have the years, but not the months or days."

"Okay, give me what you got.'

Dana read off the ages of Anthony and John Hunter at the time they committed the robbery and murdered the hostage. She told Billy she needed the names of their parents and needed to know if the parents had any other children. She also needed to know if there were death certificates on file for the parents.

"I'll try to get back to you in the morning," Billy said. "Hunter's a pretty common name so it may take longer."

Dana thanked him and hung up. Although the information she was seeking on the Hunter family was public record, there were new restrictions on obtaining that information because of the problems with identity theft that had become rampant in the last few years. Getting the information through Billy saved Dana a lot of time and red tape.

With her investigation on the Hunter murders begun, Dana decided to go through the mail Marianne had stacked on her desk. Monday's mail always included the letters that had come in on Saturday, but thankfully there were only a few new cases that needed to be assigned.

There were also two letters in the mail from readers who had been cheated by Flannery's garage thanking Globe Investigations for looking into the matter and exposing Floyd's unethical business practices.

Dana placed the letters aside for Bob and Casey to read as they had done the work on the case. She buzzed Marianne and asked if she already made copies of these letters for the file they had on Flannery.

"Yes, I did. In fact I made two copies, one for the file that went to our attorneys and another for the duplicate file I have here."

"I don't know why I asked," Dana said. "You're always a step ahead of me."

Marianne laughed. "Most of the time I'm running to catch up with you. By the way, I heard that Flannery showed up at Casey's apartment on Saturday and now he's back in jail."

"Right. Apparently our lawyers got a restraining order against him that he violated by showing up at Casey's. Bruno said he'll be in jail until the assault case goes to trial."

"Will we all have to testify?" Marianne asked.

"Of course. You're the one he actually assaulted."

"I still can't get over how Bob floored the guy. Bob may look like a big fluffy marshmallow but he's really a tough guy." The conversation, like many Dana and Marianne had when they were in the office alone, was taking place over the intercom. That way they could keep working while they talked. "Oh, hold on, Dana. I'm getting some results from my search on Mary Lou Bandini."

"I'll be right out," Dana said. She had sorted through all the mail and picked up two of the reader requests she thought Marianne could research and answer, and carried them out to the reception area.

The printer connected to Marianne's computer was cranking out the information that appeared on the screen.

Dana waited for it to finish and grabbed the paper out

of the printer. "Mary Lou Bandini is in prison for embezzlement," Dana said reading the print out. "This is too crazy."

"She's serving her second year of a five-year sentence."

"Call the prison and find out when visiting hours are and what I have to do to get permission to see her," Dana said. "Also, see if you can get transcripts from the Hunters' trial. That may give me more information than the newspaper articles."

"Greg is going back to Chicago tomorrow. I can ask him to go to the courthouse and get copies of the transcripts. It'll be faster than waiting for them to send them to us."

"I don't want to inconvenience him, but if he's willing to do it, I'll pay for his gas and food."

"I'll call him now and ask him," Marianne offered.

"Thanks. I'm going to go up to the newsroom and see Sam. I want to share some of this information with him."

Dana only spent about ten minutes with her editor. The newsroom was especially hectic that day and Sam was harried. However, Sam approved of Dana's activities and promised the paper would back her efforts.

The afternoon had passed quickly and it was close to four when Dana returned from her quick meeting with Sam. Bob and Casey showed up a few minutes later.

"We solved all four cases," Bob said proudly. "For some reason, people were very friendly and cooperative today."

"Great," Dana said. "Get your reports done and I'll look at them before I leave tonight."

"Don't you want me to tell you the details?" Bob asked. "Some of them are quite amusing."

"Don't believe him, Dana," Casey said. "All four were elderly people who have been scammed by unethical companies or individuals. It was all quite sad."

"You didn't think the guy that tried to buy a potbellied stove and got a potbellied pig instead was hilarious?"

"No. He was just dumb, and I felt sorry for the pig."

Casey suddenly looked like she might burst into tears. Dana stepped between her two investigators. "Bob, do you think you can handle the paperwork on your own? I need to discuss some things with Casey."

Both Casey and Bob had state-of-the-art laptop computers in which to input their stories. The laptops enabled them to type up their reports and if needed e-mail them straight to the newsroom for inclusion in the next edition of the *Globe*. Casey always carried her computer with her. Bob always left his at home, giving him a good excuse to go there to work.

"Don't mind at all," Bob replied cheerfully. "I'll get them done tonight and e-mail copies to all of you. None of them are front-page material, but I can condense all four into one report to warn other consumers to beware."

"Perfect," Dana said.

Casey had already left the reception area to take a seat in Dana's office. Marianne had just gotten a return call from Greg.

"Greg says he'll be glad to do it," Marianne said. "He'll bring them straight here when he comes back tomorrow."

"Wonderful. He is a great guy."

"I know it," Marianne said.

"And she owes her happiness to Bob's matchmaking service," Bob told them.

Dana and Marianne both rolled their eyes at him. Bob laughed and left the office with the day's files under his arm.

Dana joined Casey inside her private office and closed the door so they could speak privately. Casey was sitting in one of the chairs in front of Dana's desk staring at the gray skies through the window behind the desk. Her face looked as dark as the clouds that threatened to dump more snow on Crescent Hills.

"How are you doing?" Dana asked, leaning on the front of the desk to talk to Casey.

"I was pretty good all day," Casey said. "Keeping busy helps. Then, I got a call from the medical examiner's office telling me they were ready to release Tony's body to me."

"I'm sorry."

"I guess I could take him to Chicago and bury him with his brother," Casey said softly. "Only I don't know if there's any insurance or money for a funeral."

"I'm checking to see if there are any other relatives."

"I guess there could be. Everything Tony told me was a lie, including the part about not having any family. Of course, who am I to talk? I was lying like a rug too."

"You can't change the past, Casey. All you can do is move forward."

"I take it you're going to investigate Tony's murder?"

"Bruno is doing that. I'm going to work on John's murder. I don't know any of the homicide people in Chicago, and they're so overworked, they may not care if I gather some information in their case."

"Have you learned anything so far?"

"Actually, I have." Dana paused and walked behind her desk. She picked up the file folder with the articles she had printed out from the *Sun-Times* archives and handed it to Casey.

Casey looked at it without comment for a few minutes and then handed it back to Dana. "What they did was so awful. I can't believe it."

"Remember that they were young. Tony was only six-teen."

Casey nodded. "That doesn't excuse the fact that they murdered an innocent woman."

"No, it doesn't," Dana agreed. "But now we have to figure out why someone came along all these years later and murdered both of them. We need to find out more about the bank robbery victim and if she has any relatives that may have been seeking revenge."

"That works for John's murder," Casey said, "but it doesn't work for Tony. He's been out of prison for two years now."

"The newspaper articles say that the brothers got over a quarter of a million dollars in the robbery. The money was never recovered and that could be the motive behind the murders."

"Oh my God," Casey said slowly. The lost look left her face as a sudden thought sparked her enthusiasm.

"What is it?"

"I think I know where the money is, or what's left of it."

TWENTY-TWO

BRUNO CAME TO Dana's office with a death certificate for Anthony Hunter and took Casey to the bank where her late husband had a safe-deposit box.

It was almost closing time when they got to the bank but Bruno flashed his badge and said they were on urgent police business. The bank manager allowed them to enter before the doors were locked and the tellers began to close out their drawers.

Casey and Bruno were escorted back to the manager's office to conduct their business in private. The manager's name was Jim Winkleman. Dressed in a dark business suit and a crisp white shirt with a conservative gray tie, he was anxious to take care of the homicide detective, fearing that the bank might be involved in some type of criminal matter.

"Mrs. Hunter's husband passed away unexpectedly," Bruno explained. "We have a copy of the death certificate and she has a copy of her marriage license to Anthony Hunter. We would like to access the safe-deposit box Mr. Hunter had here."

Jim Winkleman's face turned pale. He obviously knew that Anthony Hunter had been a victim of foul play. "Of course. Do you also have the key?"

Bruno produced a set of keys that had been taken from Tony's pocket by the medical examiner. "I think it's one of these," he told the nervous bank manager. Bruno laid the death certificate, marriage license and set of keys on the manager's desk.

Winkleman fumbled with the keys and selected the correct one and removed it from the ring. Then, he used his computer to find the bank's record of the safe-deposit box. He handed everything back to Bruno and stood up. "Come with me, please," he said.

Casey and Bruno followed him to the area where the safe-deposit boxes were kept. Casey had not said a word since they entered the bank. She was remembering the day when she had accompanied Tony to the bank. It was the day that she had seen his Social Security card and committed the number to memory. She had used the number to try and investigate Tony's past and had not been able to find out anything of interest. It was the fingerprints on the wineglass that had uncovered Tony's past. Unfortunately, the information had come too late to keep Casey from marrying him.

Tony's reaction to learning about the master plan had planted the first seeds of doubt in Casey's mind as to why Tony had rushed her off to Las Vegas to marry him. Tony had not loved her. He had simply been after her money. Of course, the joke was on him when he found out she didn't really have any money.

"Casey?" Bruno asked. "They're ready for us."

Casey snapped out of her reverie and followed Bruno and Winkleman into the vault. Winkleman handed her Tony's key and instructed her to place it in the lock and turn it. The bank's key was then inserted into another lock and the box was slid out.

"We have private rooms you can use to open the box," Winkleman said, indicating three small rooms with solid wood doors.

"Thanks," Bruno said. "We shouldn't be too long."

Bruno carried the box and escorted Casey into the first room and closed the door. There was a table and two chairs in the room. Bruno set the box down on the table and he and Casey settled into the chairs.

Bruno waited for Casey to make a move, but she shook her head. "You open it, please," she told Bruno.

Bruno nodded and opened the lid on the long slender box. Casey held her breath, almost afraid to look at the contents of the box.

A brown leather pouch was wedged tightly into the narrow box. Bruno carefully removed it from the box and laid it on the table between them. Under the pouch were a few papers. One was the duplicate copy of Tony's Social Security card issued shortly after his release from prison. Other papers had to do with his release and the conditions of his parole.

"Open the pouch," Casey said softly.

The pouch was one that folded and was tied together with thin leather straps. It was the type of pouch you would expect a courier to use to carry valuables.

Inside the pouch were neat stacks of currency, still crisp and new despite the fact that they were more than twenty years old.

Bruno flipped through the cash. "There's only about thirty thousand dollars here, but this pouch was designed to hold a lot more than that."

"Can you trace the bills back to the bank that was robbed?"

"I don't think so. That bank went out of business years ago. As Hunter's legal wife, I'd say it belongs to you."

"I don't want it," Casey said, seemingly shocked that he would even suggest it.

"I understand, but since we haven't been able to trace

any other living relatives and technically it's not evidence, it's yours."

Casey grabbed the pouch and stuffed the money inside of it. Then, she wrapped it up in a nice neat bundle and shoved it angrily into her purse. "Fine. I'll take it," she said sullenly. "What about the papers?"

"Yours too," Bruno told her. He folded them neatly and handed them to her.

A few minutes later, much to the relief of Jim Winkleman, Bruno and Casey left the bank. The manager kept Tony's key and took the empty safe-deposit box from Bruno. He didn't ask what had been found in the box. He didn't want to know, but from the look on the young woman's face it was something that made her unhappy.

THE NEXT MORNING, Dana woke up and stretched lazily like a cat that had feasted on catnip and cream the night before. She and Bruno had managed to spend an entire evening together without any arguments.

Dinner had been a large sausage and mushroom pizza that Bruno had brought to the house. Dana's contribution had been a decadent cheesecake from Sunflower Market.

While they ate, Bruno told Dana about the trip to the bank with Casey and what had been found in Tony's safe-deposit box.

After that, they played two games of Scrabble and simply enjoyed being together and being in love. Fun evenings like that always made Dana think that their relationship was on solid ground. That lasted until the next emotional issue shook their ground like a major earthquake.

Snow had fallen the night before but it was not enough to cause any major traffic problems and Dana arrived at the office ahead of schedule.

Marianne came in a few minutes later with a box of

doughnuts. Dana had already made a pot of coffee so she and her secretary shared a continental breakfast.

"I was feeling really uneasy around Casey," Marianne admitted. "She's like a different person now, but I decided that we've been friends too long to let her slip away from me. I called her last night and she told me all about the master plan she and her two friends cooked up. I assume you already know about it."

"She told me on Saturday when she showed up on my doorstep. She had just confessed everything to Tony and he threw her out of his apartment."

"Does Bob know?"

"I haven't told anyone except Bruno and that was only because Casey asked me to tell him. She was too embarrassed to tell him herself."

"I don't think she should be embarrassed," Marianne said as she contemplated eating another doughnut. "While it was dishonest, it was rather clever, and she said both of her friends are now dating wealthy men."

"I know, but Casey got the short end of it all."

"She just picked the wrong guy," Marianne said defensively. "We all do that. Look how many good-looking snakes I've dated?"

Dana laughed. "Perhaps, but with your looks you've had your pick of males since grade school."

"I was fat and awkward in grade school," Marianne insisted.

"I was skinny and awkward," Dana admitted.

"Casey looked so good after her makeover," Marianne said. "Yesterday, she was back to her old ways and that worries me. She's lost her self-confidence again."

"She's been through a terrible trauma."

"I know."

The telephone rang and Marianne answered the phone

on Dana's desk. "Globe Investigations." She listened for a few seconds, then put the caller on hold. "It's the prison facility where Mary Lou Bandini is incarcerated. Today is visiting day and they'll put you on the list if you can get there between one and three today."

"Tell them yes," Dana instructed.

Marianne got back on the phone and relayed the message for Dana. She listened a few more minutes. "Thank you. I'll tell her."

"You're all set, but you have to bring a photo ID and submit to a search of your person and your belongings."

"No problem," Dana told her.

"Oh, and I forgot to tell you that Casey said she wouldn't be in today. She's making funeral arrangements for Tony and John too, unless someone else has stepped forward to claim his remains. She's going to use the money from the safe-deposit box to have them both cremated and their ashes interred at some place in Chicago. Under the circumstances there won't be any formal services."

The door to the outer office opened and Bob came in. "Hey, where's everyone at?" he called out.

"In here," Dana called back. "Get some coffee and come on in. We have doughnuts."

"I love you guys," he called back.

While Bob and Dana discussed his reports from yesterday's investigations, Marianne went down to the mailroom to retrieve the morning mail. Dana wanted to go through it as soon as possible since she would have to leave the office early to visit Mary Lou Bandini.

Marianne returned and sat at her desk to open the mail. Fortunately, there were only two new cases that needed to be investigated, but in a plain white envelope with a Chicago postmark there was a letter that sent Marianne running into Dana's office.

"Whoa, girl," Bob said when Marianne rushed in. "Moving that fast can make you dizzy."

Marianne ignored him. "Read this," she said, dropping the letter and the envelope in front of Dana. "But don't touch it."

Dana read the letter that looked like it had been done on a typewriter rather than a computer.

Dear Dana Sloan,
The police have arrested the wrong people in the death of Lucas Porter. They are innocent and should not be brought to trial. I am the one who killed the moron, but for obvious reasons I am not providing you with my name.

Dana read the letter aloud so Bob would know what it said.

"Oh, great," Bob said sarcastically. "Bruno and the DA will drop the charges immediately when they see that letter."

"Only Marianne touched the letter, we'll have to turn it over to the police so they can check it for other fingerprints. They'll want the envelope too, but that has probably been handled by a lot of different people."

"Bob's right," Marianne said. "I doubt if they'll pay any attention to an anonymous letter."

"Probably not, but I'm going to give it to them anyway. I'm also going to assign you to look into Lucas Porter's murder again. With all that went on with Casey, I really didn't do a thorough enough job."

"Fine with me," Bob said. "I'll go back to that sleazy pool hall and the pizza joint. Maybe I can find another witness."

"Maybe you'll find the real killer," Marianne said. "You'd better be careful."

Bob leaned over and looked at the postmark on the envelope. "According to this letter, the killer is in Chicago."

"He or she could have just mailed it from there," Dana said. "The killer could still be here in Crescent Hills."

"You never have believed that the wife and her friend did it, have you?" Bob asked.

"No. I can see why Bruno thinks they're guilty but I don't agree with him."

"Do we have any other cases to look into?" Bob asked.

"Two," Marianne said. She hurried back to her desk and returned with the two requests for help that had come in that day.

Dana read them. "These can wait a few days," she decided. "They should be fairly simple and if Casey comes back tomorrow, I can assign them to her."

"Okay," Bob said. "The pool hall and pizza place don't open until this afternoon. I'll start with the last few places Porter worked and see what I come up with."

"I'll call Bruno," Dana said. Marianne and Bob took that as their cue to leave the office.

Dana tried Bruno's desk at the station first. He laughed when Dana told him about the letter. "It's a joke, honey. You know better than to give any credence to an anonymous letter. Your newspaper tells everyone that all requests for help that come into Globe Investigations have to be signed with contact information."

"Right, and the first thing we do is check that the information is accurate."

"But you still want me to come over and get that anonymous letter and run it through the lab."

"Yes, please," Dana said sweetly. "It could be genuine."

Bruno sighed. "I'll be right over."

True to his word, Bruno showed up about five minutes later with an evidence bag to put the letter in.

"How's Casey doing?" he asked, sitting down in one of the chairs in front of Dana's desk.

"Marianne talked to her last night and I guess she's doing okay. She's not coming in today because she's making funeral arrangements for Tony and his brother too. She's going to use some of the money from Tony's safe-deposit box to pay the expenses."

"I'd say that's putting it to good use."

"It's going to take some time, but Casey is a strong girl. I think she'll be okay."

"How about lunch?" Bruno asked.

"Not today. I have an appointment in Chicago."

"Should I ask with whom?"

"No."

"Does it have something to do with Hunter's murder?"

"I don't know yet."

"Okay, sweets. As you told me the other day, my questions often start arguments and I have to get back to work. I've got a ton of paperwork to do, and I'm on duty tonight too. Just be careful and remember the bambinos."

Dana got up and pulled him out of the chair. She kissed him. "Thanks for picking up the letter," she said.

"You're welcome. Call me when you get back from your appointment."

"I will," she promised as she walked him to the door.

"Billy is on line one," Marianne said as Bruno left the office.

"Great." Dana sprinted back to her desk and picked up the phone. "Hi, Billy, what have you got?"

"Mother was Evelyn Manchester. Father was Clyde Hunter. Evelyn died in 1970."

"Her sons were both pretty young," Dana remarked.

"Right. Clyde died in 1999. I checked to see if there was another marriage on record for Clyde, but there was not and I couldn't find any other birth records listing him or Evelyn either."

"So, John and Tony had no siblings and were raised by their father."

"Yes, ma'am."

"Thanks a lot, Billy. I really appreciate it."

"You're welcome. Trudy says hello and wants you to call her to set a dinner date."

"I'll do it," Dana promised. "Thanks again."

Dana used a Post-it to write herself a note to call Trudy. She stuck it on a calendar page for the middle of next week.

Bruno's mother was coming Saturday and was supposed to stay a week. The night before, she and Bruno had talked about the possibility of taking Angelina to the farm to meet Dana's parents. Dana wasn't sure that getting their mothers together was a good idea, but she would call her mom and see what would work for her. She wrote another note and put it on the next day's calendar. Of course, once Dana told her mom that Bruno wanted Angelina to meet her family, her mom would be smelling orange blossoms and buying bridal magazines.

Marianne came into the office. "Greg just called from Chicago. He has all the transcripts from the Hunter trial. He's going to be tied up on something else the rest of the day, but he'll bring the box to my house tonight when he gets back and I'll bring it to you in the morning."

"That'll work. Thanks."

Dana went back to her office and called Casey's cell phone. Casey told her she was waiting for someone in the Chicago medical examiner's office to call her back about whether or not they could release John Hunter's body to her.

"If it helps, I found out that both of their parents are deceased and they had no siblings," Dana told her.

"I guess that makes me the closest relative," Casey said without enthusiasm.

"Listen, Casey, the real reason I called was to invite you out to dinner tonight. Bruno's working, so it'll just be the two of us."

"Thanks, Dana. I'd like that."

"I'll be out of the office the rest of afternoon, so let's pick a place and time now." Casey didn't seem to have an opinion about that, so Dana set the time at 7:00 p.m. at the Aztec Club. "We'll find a quiet booth where we can talk," Dana promised.

With that settled, Dana got her coat and scarf on and went into the reception area. She grabbed two doughnuts and wrapped them in napkins.

"You're exceeding your doughnut quota for the day," Marianne warned with a grin.

"It'll be my lunch on the way to Chicago."

"Good excuse," Marianne said as Dana went out the door.

TWENTY-THREE

BRUNO TOOK THE LETTER he had picked up from Dana's office back to the station. He called the forensics lab and told them he was bringing a piece of evidence over that he needed checked for fingerprints. Then he called Hildago's office. He knew the prosecutor was probably in court, but he left a message for him.

Jack O'Brien came into the office and sat down beside Bruno's desk. "I had to cut Hunter's cellmate loose this morning. We got nothing to hold him on."

"Did you get any useful information from the guy?"

"No. He's dumb as a rock. He saw Hunter in Las Vegas but Hunter disappeared before he had a chance to talk to him. Somehow he found out Hunter was here and came here looking for him. He said he called Hunter and Hunter told him to get lost, so he went to the bar and tied one on and then got into the fight that landed him here. He was going to call Hunter and ask him to bail him out, but by that time Hunter was dead."

"Sounds like a huge waste of time and taxpayers' money," Bruno said.

"You got that right. If the ballistics report on the Chicago murder says the bullets that killed both brothers came from the same gun, that Flannery guy who hassled Casey will be off the suspect list too. He was in jail here when the guy in Chicago was killed. So, guess what, buddy? Our list is down to one, the wife."

"Casey didn't do it," Bruno said.

"She had motive and opportunity."

"And two people who can vouch for her whereabouts at the time of the murder," Bruno told him.

"Yeah. Except those two are Casey's best friends who were in on that scheme to snag rich husbands. What did they call it, the master plan?"

"You've been reading the reports again."

"Yeah, and my point is that if those girls could think up a crazy scheme like that and actually put it into action, they could lie for a friend, or even help her kill him to get the insurance money."

"There is no insurance money in the Hunter case. You're thinking of the Porter case."

"Oh, right. Well, it doesn't matter. They thought the guy was rich and Casey would inherit his money if he died."

"Wait a minute," Bruno said becoming irritated, which happened quite frequently when he talked to Jack. "Are you saying Casey and her girlfriends got together and murdered Hunter?"

"Think about it, Bruno. It's another one of those schemes to make themselves rich. One of them kills Hunter so Casey can inherit his dough and then because they know the wife is always the primary target; they become her alibi and she becomes theirs. It's a perfect crime."

Bruno had to admit Jack had a point, but he wasn't about to give him the satisfaction of saying so. "Only one thing wrong, Jack. Hunter spent all the money he had pretending to be rich himself."

"Yeah," Jack said with a devious smile. "That's what makes the case so interesting. Everyone is after everyone else's money, only none of them really have any."

"Another of life's twisted tales," Bruno said, getting up from his desk. "And what about the brother? Do you think the girls drove to Chicago and popped him too?"

"It's possible."

"Except a witness says he saw a man going upstairs to Hunter's apartment."

Jack snorted his disapproval. "A witness who is only five years old. Come on, Bruno. You know kids aren't reliable witnesses. They'll say anything for a stick of gum."

"You're right there," Bruno admitted.

"So, I say we bring the wife and her girlfriends in for more questioning. One of them is bound to break."

"I'll think about it. In the meantime, I'm going to interview some of Hunter's friends from the country club. Maybe one of them knocked him off."

"You want me to come along?"

"No. The chief wants one of us to stay in the office to catch the calls. Today that's you."

"Sure. But think about what I've been telling you."

"I will," Bruno assured him. "By the way, I'm expecting to hear from Lou Hildago. If he calls tell him to call my cell. He's got the number."

"Will do, buddy."

Bruno put on his overcoat and picked up the evidence bag with the anonymous letter. He would drop it off at the lab on his way to the country club.

O'Brien was back at his own desk and didn't seem to notice the evidence bag and for that Bruno was grateful. He didn't want to lie to a fellow detective, but he didn't want to admit that he was having the letter checked out just to humor his girlfriend.

From the outside, the correctional facility looked like an office building rather than a jail. That image quickly disappeared once Dana entered the building. There were lots of iron bars and gates and guards with guns.

Dana waited in line with other visitors to give her name

and the name of the inmate she was visiting. She showed her driver's license to the first guard and submitted to a search by a second guard before the iron gate that separated the inspection area clicked open and she entered a corridor where another guard escorted her into the visiting area.

The room contained tables of various sizes and lots of chairs. The place was already filled with inmates and their visitors. Guards were at the door and stationed at strategic places around the room, keeping a silent watch on the inmates and their respective visitors.

"Who are you here to visit?" the female guard asked, pausing inside the doorway.

"Mary Lou Bandini," Dana replied. "I don't know what she looks like."

The guard nodded and led Dana over to a small table against the wall. A short, stout woman with black hair and a round plain face looked up at Dana. She was dressed in a royal blue jumpsuit that was tight across her ample bosom. "You my new best friend?" she asked cynically.

"I'm Dana Sloan. I'd like to talk to you about some old friends of yours."

Mary Lou motioned to the guard that she approved of the visitor and the guard left them. "Sit down, Dana Sloan," Mary Lou said.

"Thank you for seeing me," Dana said.

"Why not? This place is boring as hell and I don't get many visitors. So what do you want?"

"I want to ask you about your relationship with John and Tony Hunter."

Mary Lou shook her head. "Ancient history, girlie."

"Yes, I know, but recently both of the brothers were murdered."

"You a cop?" Mary Lou raised up in her seat, grabbing a hold of the table as if she was about to turn it over on Dana.

"No, I'm not a cop. I'm a reporter. I work for the *Globe* newspaper in Crescent Hills."

One of the guards had approached the table. "Is there a problem here?" she asked.

Mary Lou shook her head. "No problem. Everything's good," Mary Lou said.

"Then stay seated," the guard warned.

"Sure thing." Mary Lou sat down again and glared at Dana. "Look, girlie, I haven't seen those two losers in years. I thought they were both still in prison."

"Tony was released about two years ago," Dana told her. "His brother just got out last week."

"So, since they'd been guests of the state for so long, you figure someone from their wicked past did them in."

"I don't know. That may have been the case with John, but Tony has been out for a long time with no sign of trouble. In fact, Tony recently married a good friend of mine."

"She probably killed him. He was an annoying little jerk. He followed Johnny and me everywhere. I think he liked to watch us make out."

"The newspaper articles say that they were arrested at your family home. Were you hiding them after the robbery?"

"That was the plan, until I found out they killed Sarah."

"You knew Sarah?"

"Not real well, but I knew her. She was the daughter of one of my father's business associates."

"What kind of business was your father in?"

"He was a crook. Him and Sarah's old man worked together, collecting bets from losers, running numbers."

"Where are they now?"

"Pushing up daisies in Oak Park cemetery."

"Do you know why Johnny and Tony killed Sarah?"

"Yeah, I do, but I'm not in the mood to talk about it, especially to someone I don't know."

"What would get you in the mood to talk about it?" Dana asked.

"My account at the commissary doesn't have enough to buy a candy bar. A lot of visitors deposit funds in the accounts for the people they visit here."

"How much of a deposit are we talking about?" Dana asked calmly.

"Five hundred should cover it."

Dana smiled. "How about this, Mary Lou? You tell me your story and then I'll pay you what it's worth."

Mary Lou smiled back. "I like you, girlie. How about we settle on twenty bucks up front?"

Dana opened her purse and took out a twenty-dollar bill. She held it up so Mary Lou could see it, then put it back in her purse. "Let's start again. Why did the Hunter boys kill Sarah?"

"So they wouldn't have to split the dough with her."

"She was in on the robbery?"

"Of course. She planned the whole thing. Johnny and Tony couldn't plan a trip to the beach on their own. She went inside the bank first and pretended to be their hostage so they'd have a better chance of getting away. Sarah was older than us and had been fooling around with the assistant manager, some geeky guy about ten years older than she was. That's how Sarah knew they had a lot of extra money in the drawers on Fridays because people came in and cashed their paychecks. Then, according to Johnny, after they got away Sarah wanted to take possession of the cash bag. They got into a fight about it and one of them shot her in the head."

Dana sat back in her chair. "Do you have a name for the geeky assistant manager?"

"Sarah used to call him Stu the Stud. I don't know what his last name was."

"Did Sarah's involvement in the robbery or her relationship with the bank manager come out at the trial?"

Mary Lou looked at her. "No one knew about it except me and the boys and Sarah. They might have told their lawyer, but he was one of those public defenders who didn't know which end was up. Same kind of jerk that landed me in here."

"Did you testify at the trial?"

"I had to, but I don't remember what I said. It was a long time ago and I was scared the boys might get off and come after me."

"For turning them in to the police? Did you get a reward?"

"What makes you think it was me who turned them in?"

"Wasn't it?"

Mary Lou grinned. "Yeah, it was. To tell the truth, I wasn't really after the reward money, it was peanuts. It was the bank loot I wanted, but I underestimated the boys. After they killed Sarah they hid the money somewhere and would never tell anyone, not me, not the cops, nobody, where it was. If Tony got out of prison two years ago, he probably got to it first and spent it all."

"All but about thirty thousand dollars," Dana told her.

"In that case, maybe Johnny killed him."

"I don't think so," Dana said. "I'm working on the assumption that the two murders are connected. Do you know anything else about the bank manager Sarah was dating?"

"No. He was supposedly home sick the day of the robbery, so I don't know if they even called him to testify.

I've always wondered if the real plan wasn't for Sarah to get the money from Johnny and Tony and run off with her boyfriend."

"What makes you think that?"

"I don't know," she said with a shrug. "Like I said, I wasn't real close with Sarah. I guess I just knew that she thought John and Tony were dummies and she could get them to do the dirty work and she'd reap the rewards."

"What about Clyde Hunter? John and Tony's father?"

"He was so drunk most of the time he didn't know what they were up to. He didn't even come to the trial."

"Is there anyone else you can think of that might have had a reason to want John and Tony dead? Relatives of Sarah's maybe?"

"Just me, but as you can see, I got an iron-clad alibi."

"You seem like a smart woman," Dana said. "How'd you end up in here?"

"My boss was such an idiot, he made it easy for me to steal from him. The problem was I got greedy and started taking more and more. Greed is a dangerous thing."

"Yes, it is," Dana agreed.

"Well, the good thing about doing a white-collar crime is that you get sent to a place like this. Me and Martha Stewart got that in common."

A voice came over a loud speaker announcing that visiting hours would be over soon. Mary Lou called out for one of the guards to come over to them.

"My friend, here, wants to donate to my commissary fund," she told him. "I need a slip from you."

The guard pulled a pad and pen from his shirt pocket. Mary Lou explained that Dana had to sign the slip and give the money to the guard, who would then put it in Mary Lou's account.

"How much are you donating?" the guard asked Dana.

"Forty dollars," Dana said, pulling two twenties from her purse and handing it to him.

"Thanks," Mary Lou said.

"Here's my card, Mary Lou," Dana said handing it to her. "Let me know if you think of anything else."

"You got the whole story, girlie. There isn't any more to tell."

TWENTY-FOUR

CASEY WAS ALREADY AT the Aztec Club when Dana arrived. She was seated in a booth toward the back, away from the main lights of the restaurant and the television set that hung on the wall behind the bar area.

"How are you doing?" Dana asked as she slid into the booth across from her friend.

"I'm getting better," Casey replied. "I arranged for a funeral home here to cremate—" She stopped. It was obviously still hard for Casey to say his name. "The man here was very nice and helpful. He will transfer the ashes here to a crematorium he knows in Chicago that will take care of John. Their ashes will be interred in the same niche at a Chicago cemetery. There will be no services and I won't have to do anything but pay the bills."

"I think that's probably for the best," Dana told her. "You've done all you can now for both of them and you have to start thinking of yourself again and moving forward."

"Sure," Casey said with a forced smile. "I'm going to do that."

Casey's appearance was better than it had been in the office yesterday. She had fixed her hair and applied makeup so that her pale features had some color. The outfit she wore was one that Marianne had helped her pick out too.

"You look good, Casey," Dana said sincerely. "That's the first step toward recovery."

"Thanks. So, tell me about your appointment in Chicago. I'm assuming it had something to do with one of the murders."

"Actually, it had to do with both of them. I went to the Illinois Correctional Facility for Women to visit a woman who knew the Hunter brothers at the time of the bank robbery."

"Who was she?"

"She was John's girlfriend at the time. They were hiding out at her family home and she was the one who turned them in to the police."

"Did she tell you why?"

"Yes. Let's order some food and I'll tell you the whole story."

Dana signaled for the waitress and they ordered dinner salads, roast-beef sandwiches and soft drinks. Then Dana related her experience with Mary Lou that afternoon and told Casey everything she had learned from the woman.

"That doesn't really confirm our theory that someone from their past killed them for revenge."

"No, but it doesn't rule it out, either. Greg picked up the trial transcripts for me today and maybe something will turn up in there."

"Well, this sounds awful," Casey said, "but the fact that Sarah Turner actually masterminded the robbery and might have been planning to take off with all the money makes me feel a little better. At least I can tell myself that Tony didn't murder an innocent person in cold blood."

"True." Dana didn't say that robbing a bank and then shooting your accomplice was still pretty bad. It all stemmed from greed, as Mary Lou said earlier, a dangerous thing.

"I'm going to use the balance of the stolen money to pay off the loan that Carmen, Cathy and I took out to make me look wealthy. Making that payment every month would just remind me of how stupid I was to take part in a scheme like that. I'm also going to quit the country club. To tell you the truth, I didn't really enjoy going there all that much."

By the time they had finished eating, Dana felt that Casey was going to be all right. Unfortunately, that was just about the time that Jack O'Brien came into the Aztec Club.

Casey saw him first. "Oh, no. Jack O'Brien just walked in. I hope he doesn't see us."

Dana agreed, but both of them were disappointed when O'Brien came directly to their table.

"Hello, ladies," he said pleasantly. "I hope you're not planning another one of those master plans."

"Get lost, Jack," Dana told him bluntly.

"I guess you're still mad because I called Bruno and told him you were at a murder scene."

"No. I just don't like you," she said with a smile.

Jack turned to Casey. "How about you, Mrs. Hunter? Do you dislike me too?"

"I don't know you well enough for that," Casey said.

"Well, guess what? I'm working on the murder of your husband and you're going to get to know me pretty well. In fact, I may become your worst nightmare."

"Let's go, Casey," Dana said, standing up and grabbing her coat. O'Brien was blocking their way. "Get out of the way, Jack, or I'll start screaming."

Jack laughed and backed away, putting his hands in the air as a sign of surrender. "Sorry. I didn't mean to upset you, Dana. I'll see you around."

Dana and Casey hurried past him and went out the door to the parking lot next door where their windshields had become frosted in the cold night air.

"He thinks I killed Tony," Casey said when they reached her car.

"Bruno is the lead detective on the case, and he knows you didn't, so don't let O'Brien worry you."

"I'll try not to, but these days everything upsets me."

"I know," Dana said, giving her a hug. "But it will get better."

"Thanks for being such a good friend," Casey said as she used her credit card to scrape frost off her windshield.

"It works both ways," Dana said. "Be careful going home."

Dana hurried over to her car, got in and started the engine, then turned on the defroster. While she waited for the windshield to clear, she got out her cell phone and dialed Bruno's number.

"Hi, sweetheart," he said with a warmth in his voice that took the chill out of the air. "Where are you?"

"I'm in the parking of the Aztec Club waiting for my car window to defrost. I had dinner with Casey and your partner O'Brien came in and upset both of us."

"What did he do?" Bruno asked with an edge to his voice.

"First he accused us of plotting another master plan, a very sore subject with Casey, and then he accused her of killing her husband."

"I'll have a talk with him tomorrow," Bruno said.

"He was just spouting off, wasn't he?" Dana asked. "You know that Casey couldn't kill anyone."

Bruno sighed. "What about those two girlfriends of hers?"

"What about them?"

"Do you think they could have had something to do with Tony's death?"

"Is that one of Jack's theories?"

"Yes, but I'm afraid the way he tells it, it makes sense."

"That's ridiculous," Dana said angrily. "You can't possibly believe that."

"I don't believe it, but I can't stop O'Brien from double-checking everyone's alibi."

"I am so sorry I called you," Dana said. She clicked off the telephone and then turned it off so Bruno couldn't call her back.

Her windshield had cleared. The car engine had warmed, and Dana was hot. She put the car in gear and drove out of the lot and headed toward her apartment, muttering to herself.

While she understood that Bruno had to do his job, she was now frightened that Casey and her friends could be facing the same type of situation that had landed Judy Porter and Teddy Larson in jail.

Dana parked her car and quickly ran up the stairs to her apartment. The telephone was ringing, but Dana ignored it thinking it was Bruno. She really had to invest in caller ID.

After shedding her coat and scarf and hanging everything neatly in the closet, Dana checked for phone messages. There were none. Whoever had been calling when she came through the door had just hung up.

Dana went into the kitchen and made herself a cup of herbal tea. Then she picked up the phone and called the one person in her life who could always cheer her up, her mom.

No matter what time of the day or night she called her mother, Linda Sloan always sounded like hearing from Dana was the best thing that happened all day.

"You sound down, honey," her mom said after they had exchanged a few words.

"It's been a rough few weeks," Dana said and then proceeded to explain all that had happened with Casey.

"Poor Casey. She must be devastated," Linda said.

"She was doing better until Detective Jack O'Brien showed up tonight and gave us a hard time. He thinks Casey and her friends murdered Tony Hunter."

"That's just stupid," Linda said. "What does Bruno think?"

"Bruno said he can't stop O'Brien from double-checking their alibis. He made me so mad, I hung up on him."

"I'm sure he didn't mean to upset you, dear," her mom said.

"He never means to upset me," Dana retorted. "But he does it all the time."

"And you never upset him?" her mother asked.

Dana couldn't help smiling. "Okay, you're right. I upset him too."

"Every couple has their ups and downs," Linda said. "It's your ability to forgive and forget that's important. I forgive your father at least three times a day."

Dana laughed. "Dad is a prince and you know it."

They talked awhile longer and Dana got updated on all that was going on in the farming community and in the lives of her brothers and their families. "When are you coming to visit?" her mom finally asked. "We miss you."

"Actually Bruno's mother is coming here next week and we were thinking of bringing her to the farm to meet my family."

"Oh, that would be wonderful. I'd love to meet her."

"What would be a good time for you and dad?"

"Anytime you can make it, Dana. Just give me a few hours' notice."

Dana promised she would and they said their good-byes. Dana hung up the phone and it rang immediately.

Since the chat with her mom had improved her disposition she answered the phone even though she thought it was Bruno. It wasn't.

"Dana? It's Casey. I hope I'm not calling too late."

"No problem. I just got off the phone with my mom."

"I'm worried about Carmen and Cathy. Bruno was really cool when he questioned them, but if O'Brien starts hassling them, I don't know how they'll take it."

"It may not come to that," Dana assured her. "The Chicago police are running a ballistics test on the bullets fired at John's apartment. If it matches with the tests run on the bullet from Tony's apartment, it will confirm that the murders are related, and there is a witness that saw a man go up to Hunter's apartment right before Sam and I got there."

"Didn't you say the witness was a child?"

"Yes, but that doesn't mean we can discount what he saw."

"Does Bruno believe that?"

"I don't know, but I spoke with him after we left the Aztec Club and told him that O'Brien was giving us a hard time. I think he'll talk to Jack and convince him to wait for the ballistics report."

"Which could make O'Brien think that we murdered both brothers," Casey replied.

"Casey," Dana said firmly. "You've been through the worst kind of traumas and your emotions are totally raw. You've dealt with Jack O'Brien before and you know that he's ninety percent smoke and mirrors, so don't give so much weight to what he said tonight. I think he was just showing off."

Casey sighed. "You're right. Every little thing that happens throws me into a panic these days."

"And whatever happens, we'll deal with it together."

"Thanks, Dana. That's why I called you. I can always count on you to make me feel better."

The call ended with Dana thinking that maybe some of her mother's ability to cheer and comfort others had rubbed off on her.

Her doorbell rang several times in a row. There was only one person who leaned on the bell that way. Dana went to let Bruno in.

TWENTY-FIVE

"I DID TALK TO ONE GUY who said the pool hall was usually frequented by the same people every night, but on the night that Lucas Porter disappeared there was a guy in there that he had never seen before," Bob told Dana over lunch the next day. "He also said he thought the guy left about the same time that Porter left."

"Did he give you a description?"

"Not one that will help much," Bob replied. "Medium height, medium build, didn't get a good look at his face because he stayed at the bar the whole time with his head down. He did say the guy was dressed in black and kept his hat on the whole time."

Casey had called to say she wouldn't be in until the afternoon. Dana wondered if she hadn't been up most of the night worrying about Jack O'Brien and his accusations.

Marianne had gone out to lunch with her friends from the circulation department. Bob and Dana had ordered sandwiches from the coffee shop in the lobby of the building. Bob had been out looking into a new case that had come into the *Globe* via e-mail late the previous afternoon, and this was the first chance he and Dana had to talk about the Porter case.

Dana finished chewing a piece of the tuna-fish sandwich she had ordered and looked at Bob quizzically. "What kind of hat?"

"A black cap with an Arizona Cardinals logo on it."

Dana thought about that for a moment and suddenly

remembered what the football team's logo was. "The Arizona Cardinals' logo is a red bird, a cardinal."

"That's right."

"Oh, my," Dana said, dropping her sandwich onto the paper plate on her desk. "The little boy who saw the man go up to Hunter's apartment said the man was wearing a black hat with red bird on it."

"No kidding?"

"I guess it could just be a coincidence, but most of the people here and in Chicago are Bears fans. They wouldn't be caught dead in a Cardinals hat."

"That could mean the murder of Lucas Porter and John Hunter are connected."

"Do you think it's possible that they even knew each other?"

"It's a long shot, but worth asking Judy Porter about. I'll call her after lunch," Dana said. "How come the guy you talked to yesterday didn't offer this information the last time you went in there?"

"He wasn't there that afternoon." Bob looked at his notes. "His name is Walter Connors. He works at some computer store and sometimes has to work until nine. Yesterday was his day off."

"What about the bartender? Did he remember the guy with the Cardinals hat?"

"He's the owner of the place and says he doesn't remember anyone like that. To be honest, I think he drinks more than any of his customers so he probably wouldn't remember if Michael Jordan came in that night."

The telephone rang and Dana picked it up. "Globe Investigations."

"What are you doing for lunch?" Bruno asked.

"Bob and I ordered sandwiches. We had some cases to talk over."

"I won't ask which ones," he said.

"Thank you," Dana replied.

"I just called to tell you we got the ballistics report from Chicago. It matches our report, so both of the Hunters were killed with bullets from the same gun. Now all we have to do is find the person who owns the gun."

"Did you talk to O'Brien?"

"Yes, and I told him everything you told me to tell him."

"I doubt that, but now that you have the ballistics report, he has to admit that Casey and her friends are no longer suspects in either case."

"That would be a big concession for O'Brien."

"Bruno, Sam and I were at John Hunter's murder scene. He was killed by a man."

"You told me that last night and you told me to tell O'Brien that, so I did. I'll call you later, love."

Bruno hung up. Dana turned her attention back to Bob, telling him about the results of the two ballistics reports.

"I take it that didn't convince O'Brien to lay off Casey and her girlfriends."

"I guess not, but I don't have time to worry about him now."

"What about the anonymous letter we got in the Porter case. Did Bruno run it through the lab?"

"He said he took it over there personally, but it's not a priority so it may be a while before we get any results. He did say he talked to Louis Hildago about it and he laughed like a loon."

"What about Troy Kimball? Does he know about it?"

"I don't know. I guess we should have sent him a copy, but I didn't want to take a chance of messing it up by putting it in the copier. I'll call him right after I talk to Judy Porter."

Bob stood up. "I'm going back to the three places where Porter worked to ask some more questions, unless something else came in here that I have to check out."

"No. All the other requests that came in today can be handled by Marianne except for one." Dana picked up a letter. "I'm saving this one for Casey."

Bob took it and scanned it. "Aaron Bloomfield's cat is missing again. You're right. Casey will want to handle this one."

Aaron Bloomfield contacted Globe Investigations every few weeks or so. He was ninety-six years old and had outlived all of his relatives. Each time he wrote, either Casey or Bob would pay him a visit. Aaron always said his cat was missing, but Aaron lived in a nursing home and didn't have a cat. His real problem was that he was lonesome and wanted someone to listen to his stories about being a stuntman for the movies and dating all the beautiful actresses.

Marianne returned from lunch and Casey came in a short time later. Casey was soon on her way to visit Aaron Bloomfield. She offered to stop back at the office when she was done to see if any other cases had come in.

"Whatever comes in this afternoon can be dealt with tomorrow," Dana told her. "Spend as much time with Aaron as you'd like."

Marianne was amazed to find out that Bruno had been the only phone call that had come in while she was at lunch. "It's really been slow," she told Dana.

"Thank goodness," Dana replied. "I have two phone calls to make and then I want to get back to the trial transcripts Greg delivered."

"It won't take me too long to take care of the research I have," Marianne said. "I'll be glad to help you when I'm done."

"I'll be glad to have you help me," Dana said. "Most

of this stuff is so boring, I have to read it standing up so I don't nod off."

Marianne turned to her computer and her research and Dana went to her desk to make her phone calls. Judy's voice reflected the stress that she was under, but she said that she was happy to hear from Dana and even happier to hear that Bob was looking into the case again. However, Judy said she didn't know anyone who might wear an Arizona Cardinals hat and then admitted that she didn't know what their logo looked like anyway. She was positive that Lucas didn't know either of the Hunter brothers.

Troy Kimball was out of his office, but Dana left a message with his secretary about the anonymous letter her office had received.

With the phone calls done, Dana picked up the trial transcripts again.

AFTER FAILING TO COME UP with any new information at the temp office or the two temporary places of employment where Lucas Porter had worked before his death, Bob decided to stop by the Sunflower Market and see if he could talk to the manager or Porter's coworker in the stockroom.

The store was busy and the manager said he didn't have time to talk. "Besides, I told that curly headed woman everything I know about Lucas Porter." Just then, his name was announced over the loud speaker. "Another crisis," he muttered as he hurried away from Bob.

Bob strolled over to the bakery case and bought two chocolate chip cookies to boost his morale and his energy level. He munched on the cookies as he made his way back to the stockroom to see if he could find Jose.

The only one in the stockroom was George, who was

loading some cartons onto a cart. Like everyone else who shopped at Sunflower Market, Bob knew George.

"Hey, George," Bob said. "I'm looking for Jose. Is he here?"

George looked up. "He called in sick today. In fact several people called in sick so we're shorthanded."

"That's why the manager was so harried," Bob said.

"I guess. Can I help you with something?"

"Maybe. I know Dana talked to you a few weeks ago about Lucas Porter. Anything you forgot to tell her about him?"

"He beat up his wife. I guess that's why she killed him."

"How did you know he abused his wife?"

"Lucas brought her in here to shop once a week. He always acted real nice with her, but you'd have to be blind not to notice the bruises the girl had on her."

Bob nodded. "Anything else you can tell me?"

"That cookie you're eating has three hundred calories."

"For one cookie?"

"Yes, sir."

"Well, I guess that's why it tastes so good. See you, George."

Bob returned to the office to find both Dana and Marianne reading the trial transcripts.

"I came up with zero on the Porter case today," Bob told them. "How are you guys doing?"

"I never knew that people could talk so much without really saying anything," Marianne said.

"Must be all females you're reading about," Bob quipped.

Both girls refused to give him the satisfaction of a reply. "We had some new inquiries come in via e-mail," Dana said. "Here's the printouts on the ones that will need looking into."

Bob took the pages she handed him and settled himself into the other chair by her desk. "By the way, I went past Flannery's Garage and the building is for sale."

"He probably has to sell it to pay his legal fees," Dana said absently. "So you didn't learn anything new about Porter's case today?"

"Just that George thinks Mrs. Porter killed her husband because he was abusing her."

"Hey," Marianne said suddenly. "Here's a reference to that bank manager. His name is Stuart Hollingsworth. It's testimony that Sarah Turner's father was giving."

"What does it say?" Dana asked.

"He said, 'My daughter was engaged to the manager there, Stu Hollingsworth. I'm sure that's why she was in the bank that day. She didn't know he had called in sick that day.' And then the lawyer said, 'Are you referring to the assistant manager, Stuart G. Hollingsworth?' and Turner said that was him."

"Okay, at least now we have a name. What else did it say about him?"

"That was it. The father just talked about how beautiful and sweet his daughter was. He started crying and the judge excused him."

"Do you want me to run Hollingsworth through my database programs?"

"Please."

Marianne got up and went back to her desk. Dana looked at Bob, who was waiting patiently to be noticed. "So, all we've come up with so far is the guy in the Cardinals hat?"

Bob nodded. "I also learned that the chocolate chip cookies at Sunflower bakery have three hundred calories each."

"Who told you that?"

"George, of course. He's the only one who would talk to me today. The manager said he was too busy, and that Jose who works in the stockroom with Porter was out sick."

"Okay," Dana said. "I guess I'll call Kimball back and tell him about the guy in the hat and let him take it from there. Do you have the contact information for the witness?"

Bob reached in his jacket pocket and pulled out his notebook. He flipped through a few pages and then tore two of them out and handed them to Dana. "That's Connors's address and home phone and what he told me about the guy at the bar."

"I'll have Marianne type it up and we can fax it over to Kimball's office. I'm sure he'll want to interview this guy himself and probably call him as a witness."

"What about the possibility that the guy at the bar is the same guy that killed John Hunter in Chicago?"

"Judy Porter says she's sure that Lucas didn't know either of the Hunter brothers so I don't see how it could be connected."

"It was a long shot," Bob replied. "Well, I'm going to get started on these new inquiries. The day is still young." Bob eased himself out of the chair as Marianne returned. "I'll see you and Greg for dinner tonight," he said to Marianne as he left.

"Right. See you later," she called after him.

"Dinner with the in-laws?" Dana asked with a grin.

"Yes. It's become a weekly thing," she replied.

"Nice. What did you get on Hollingsworth?"

"He left Chicago right after the trial and moved to Arizona, where he sold real estate and brokered mortgages. I called the real estate office and they said he retired a few years ago and they lost track of him."

"He doesn't seem like much of a suspect," Dana said.

"Except he lived in Arizona where the Cardinals play, so he could have the team's hat."

"Him and thousands of other fans," Marianne said. "Now what?"

"Back to the transcripts to see if any other names turn up," Dana replied. "But first, I'd like you to type up the notes Bob made on the Porter case so we can fax the information to Kimball's office. I'll call and let him know it's coming."

TWENTY-SIX

BY THE BEGINNING OF the following week the weather had become unseasonably warm for the end of February.

Both Hunter brothers had been cremated and interred at a Chicago cemetery. Casey had hired a company to clean out Tony's apartment and pack up all the contents. The boxes and all the furniture were then donated to the Salvation Army. The money from the safe-deposit box along with a small amount of cash that had been found at Tony's apartment was used to pay off the loans the three Cs had taken out to put the master plan into action. There was less than a thousand dollars left after that and Casey gave it to Lucille as a donation for the new children's wing at the hospital.

Casey was back to work full time and since their caseload had suddenly increased, Dana was happy to have her.

"What are you wearing to the benefit tomorrow night?" Marianne asked Dana as they prepared to close up the office on Wednesday night.

"I'm going out now to look for a new dress," Dana told her. "It's been so busy this week, I haven't even had time to think about it. What are you wearing?"

"I don't know. Greg just came up with these tickets at the last minute. Maybe I should come shopping with you."

"That would be great. We can stop for dinner too, unless you have plans with Greg."

"He's working at the youth center tonight. Where's Bruno?"

"He drove to Chicago to pick up his mother."

"I can't wait to meet her. What do you think she'll wear?"

"Bruno said she'd wear a black dress. It seems that when Italian women lose their husbands, the widows wear black for the rest of their lives."

"I think that's pretty old-fashioned. Has she worn black every time you've seen her in the past?"

"I don't remember," Dana replied. "Mrs. Bruno is one of those women who is larger than life, and you get so caught up in listening to her that she could be wearing a potato sack and you wouldn't notice."

"So you like her?" Marianne asked.

"I do, but I also feel a bit lost when I'm with her. Come to think of it, sometimes I feel the same way about her son."

Marianne laughed. "Except when you're wrapping him around your little finger."

"Please," Dana said, rolling her hazel eyes. "If his mother weren't coming today, we wouldn't even be speaking to each other.'

"Is he still upset about you helping Troy Kimball with the Porter case?"

"Yes. And I'm upset about his failure to get Jack O'Brien to back off of Casey and her friends. He's been hounding them so much, the guys Carmen and Cathy were dating split."

"Well, since the master plan seems to have failed so miserably, they'll have to see if Bob can help them. He's still bugging Casey to go out with his mechanic friend."

"I don't think Casey is ready to start dating again," Dana said with a note of sadness in her voice.

The telephone rang. Dana and Marianne both looked at it and then at each other. "Let it ring. The service will pick it up. You and I have some serious shopping to do."

The girls pulled on their coats and headed for the door.

BRUNO GOT THE answering machine at Dana's office and hung up without leaving a message. His five-year-old nephew, Ricky, was sitting on the sofa next to him.

"Who are you calling, Uncle Al?"

"My friend, Dana, but she wasn't there."

"Mommy says you're going to marry her."

"Maybe," Bruno said absently.

"Of course you're going to marry her." Angelina Bruno had stepped into the room wheeling her suitcase behind her. "She's the perfect girl for you."

"I don't think she shares that opinion," Bruno told her.

"She doesn't have to agree with my opinion, but I know a good match for you when I see one. She's the first girl you've ever dated that didn't just swoon over your big strong body and your handsome face and let you take charge of the relationship. Dana is a lovely girl and she probably has lots of good-looking men after her, but more importantly she is smart and secure and doesn't let you tell her what to do or how to live her life."

"That's for sure," Bruno replied.

"Are you arguing with her again?"

"Actually, I was calling her now to avoid an argument on one of my cases that she's insisted on butting into."

"I see. We'll discuss it in the car," Angelina said firmly, looking at Ricky who was listening to every word of their conversation. Her son was a homicide detective so all of his cases involved some type of violence, and she didn't want Ricky to hear such things.

Bruno nodded. "What time are we going to dinner?"

"We should leave now. The reservations are for six and with traffic, it will take time for us to get there. Come on, Ricky. We have to get your jacket and hat on."

"I can do it myself, Grandma," Ricky said, sliding off the sofa and walking past her.

"I know you can, but Grandma likes to help you." Angelina followed her grandson into the extra bedroom.

Bruno took out his cell phone and dialed Dana's cell phone number. She answered on the third ring. "Hi, sweets. Did you leave the office early?"

"A little. Marianne and I decided to go shopping for something to wear to the charity dinner tomorrow night. Where are you?"

"At my mom's place. We're meeting my sisters and their husbands and kids for dinner. Then, Mom and I will drive to Crescent Hills. I hope that cleaning crew did a good job on my apartment."

"I'm sure it's fine," Dana said. "Why did you call the office?"

"I wanted to tell you that one of the lab guys called me and said they did get a print off that letter. It's too large to be a woman's print, so I don't think it belongs to you or Marianne. Did Bob or any other man touch it?"

"No. Marianne is the only one who touched it when she took it out of the envelope and read it. After that we handled it like any piece of evidence."

"Good. I've got the lab running it through all the databases we can access. I'll let you know if we get any kind of match."

"Okay. Thanks. Enjoy your dinner and say hello to everyone for me."

"I will. By the way, my mother just told me that you are the perfect woman for me."

Considering the arguments they'd had lately, Dana wasn't sure how to respond to that. "Marianne is waving at me," she said. "I think she found some good dresses on the sale rack. We can talk about that later with your mom."

Bruno laughed. "I'll hold you to it."

They said their good-byes and Bruno hung up just as Ricky and Angelina emerged from the bedroom. Both of them were dressed for the cold weather outside.

Bruno put on his coat and picked up his mother's suitcase.

"Where's your hat?" his mother asked.

"I don't need one. We'll be in the car."

"What did you do with the hat I bought you for Christmas?"

"I don't wear it because it makes me look like a roaring twenties gangster."

"You look like one anyway," Angelina said with a grin.

"Dana said the same thing," Bruno told her. "Have you two been plotting things behind my back?"

"Not yet."

"What's a gangster?" Ricky asked.

"Ask your mother," Bruno told him.

JUDY PORTER STOOD in front of her latest painting and studied it carefully. It needed something, but she wasn't sure what. Her mind was so muddled these days that she had a hard time deciding what to eat for breakfast. In the past, she had always been able to find peace and solace in her work. She understood now that it had been the way she had escaped from the cruel reality of life with Lucas.

Lucas had dominated her and made her believe that she was worthless. She stayed with him year after year because he had convinced her that she wouldn't be able to function without him.

"You're not smart enough to live on your own," Lucas had told her over and over. "You wouldn't be able to get yourself paintbrushes without me. There's no one in the world that loves you like I do. There's no one else who would take care of you like I do. Any other husband would expect you to go out and get a job to help with the bills. Where would your dreams of being a famous painter be then? Down the toilet, that's where," he'd say softly.

Judy believed him and the first weeks without Lucas to lean on were awful. She didn't know how to function without him, and then just when she found out that life without Lucas could be good, even wonderful, she had been arrested for his murder. The guilt washed over her again, so strong that she staggered away from the painting on the easel and went to sit down on the sofa again.

The guilt she felt wasn't so much for herself as it was for Teddy. Dear sweet Teddy had been her friend. He had nursed her bruises and helped her in so many little ways. Now because of her, he was in danger of losing his freedom.

Judy didn't know if she would be able to handle prison, but she was sure that someone like Teddy, with his soft blond looks, would be destroyed by prison life.

There was a knock on the door. Judy pushed herself up and went to see who was there. Teddy had installed a chain lock on her door so she could open it just enough to see who was standing in the hallway. All the publicity she had gotten made her sought after by reporters and curiosity seekers.

The chain was already in place so Judy opened the door a crack and saw Teddy standing in the hallway with a big smile on his face. "Let me in, Judy. I have good news."

Judy closed the door to disengage the chain and then opened it again to admit Teddy. He was dressed in his work clothes. Teddy had feared that he would lose his job when he was indicted for murder, but his boss believed in his innocence and kept him on. He even found work for Teddy to do in the office of the hardware store to keep him off the sales floor and away from public scrutiny.

"What's the news?" Judy asked impatiently.

"Hold on," he said. "My mom is coming over and I want to tell you both at the same time."

A soft rap on the door signaled the arrival of Sally Larson. Teddy let her in and instructed her and Judy to sit down on the worn sofa. Teddy stood in front of them, still grinning.

"Tell us already," his mom said.

"Okay. Here it is. You know I'm working in the office now, helping the bookkeeper, Maureen. She's got this fabulous computer system that tracks all the sales and the inventory and stuff. Anyway, today we were talking and I said the fact that the hammer that killed Lucas was one that we sold in our store looked real bad for us. Maureen asked what day Lucas was killed and I told her, so she does this search on the computer for that day and a few days prior to it and comes up with sales receipts for that particular hammer, and there was only one receipt for the day that Lucas disappeared. That hammer is not one of our best sellers." Teddy stopped and grinned again.

"Go on, Teddy," his mother prompted.

"Anyway, we looked at the receipt and it turns out Lucky sold the hammer. Lucky is one of those guys who talks to everyone. When the store is busy, Mr. Hillman always tells Lucky to sell more and talk less. So, Maureen calls Lucky into the office and shows him the receipt and asks him if he remembers anything about the customer that bought the hammer. And bingo! Lucky says he does because he asked the guy what he needed it for and the guy said some home repairs and Lucky told him he should buy a smaller hammer because the one he chose was too big for most jobs. The guy insisted that this was the hammer he wanted so Lucky sold it to him."

"I don't understand," Judy said. "How does that help us?"

"It helps because Lucky remembers that the guy was wearing a hat with an Arizona Cardinals logo and he asked him if he was from Arizona and the guy said he lived there for a while and used to go to the games."

"Is that a baseball team?" his mother asked.

"No," Judy said jumping to her feet. "It's a football team and Dana Sloan called me a few days ago and asked me if Lucas knew any Arizona Cardinal fans. Then she sent our lawyer some information on a guy her investigator talked to at the pool hall who remembered a guy in an Arizona Cardinals hat in the pool hall the night Lucas was killed."

"Oh my God," Sally said, catching some of Judy's excitement. "This could be very important. We have to call your lawyer right away."

"First I'm going to call Dana," Judy said.

DANA AND MARIANNE were having dinner at Marsella's. Dana hadn't been there since the night she and Bruno had dinner with Casey and Tony. They were talking about how that dinner had led to them finding out about Tony's past when Judy Porter called.

TWENTY-SEVEN

THE NEXT MORNING, Dana went straight to her editor's office to fill him in on the new developments in the Porter case.

"If nothing else," Sam said after he heard the story, "it will allow Kimball to present reasonable doubt to the jury."

"Yes, and we still have the possibility of tracing the fingerprint on the anonymous letter to someone."

"I wouldn't put too much faith in that, Dana. Most letters like that come from cranks."

"I know that. We get them all the time, but with nothing else to go on in the case, I think it's worth checking out."

"You're right. Keep me posted."

Dana took the elevator up to her own office. Marianne was going through the morning mail and there appeared to be a lot of it.

"I'm sorry I said anything about it being slow," Marianne said. "Bruno called and wants you to call him on his cell."

Dana hurried into her office and hung up her outer garments before sitting behind her desk and reaching for the phone.

"Good morning," she said when Bruno answered.

"Hi, sweets," he replied. "My mother wants to go to the mall this morning and look for a dress for the dinner tonight. You got any suggestions?"

"Marianne and I both found dresses at Terrell's but that

may be a little young for her taste. Have her try Gordon's. My mom always goes there when she's in town. Can I say hello to her?"

"No. She's cleaning my kitchen."

"I thought the service did that yesterday."

"They did, but not to my mother's liking. Are you free for lunch?"

"I don't think I'm going to get lunch today," Dana said. "We've got stacks of regular mail and e-mails to go through and Marianne and I both want to leave early to get dressed for the big dinner tonight. It starts at seven you know."

"If you say so. Okay, we'll pick you up at six-thirty."

"How was your dinner last night?"

"My sisters are both turning into clones of my mom. They say the same things to their kids that Ma used to say to us. It's uncanny."

"Anything turn up on that fingerprint yet?"

"No. I'll call you if I hear anything."

Bruno clicked off and Dana looked through the other phone messages Marianne had placed on her desk. One of them was from Troy Kimball and Dana decided to return the call before Bob and Casey came in for the staff meeting.

The dress that Dana purchased for the dinner at Ventana was a deep burgundy with a jeweled neckline and three-quarter-length sleeves. It had tiny pleats that started just below the bodice and then fell gracefully to the hemline. Dana was grateful that all the snow had melted so she could wear the black stiletto heels that made her feel tall and slinky. She wore the simple strand of pearls that had been her mother's with the matching pearl earrings.

By the time Dana had put the finishing touches on her hair and makeup, her doorbell was ringing. She took a deep breath and went to answer it.

Bruno was standing in the hallway alone. He looked at her in the dress and motioned for her to spin around. When she did, he whistled his appreciation.

"You look spectacular," he said.

"Where's your mom?"

"In the car. She said she'll give you a proper hug when we get to the hotel, but I want to give you one now."

"Okay, but don't wrinkle the dress," Dana said.

Bruno pulled her into his arms and if the dress had not been made of a wrinkle-free fabric, the pleats would have been flattened. "Shopping with my mom all day was awful. Next time you take her."

Dana laughed. "I give you credit for taking her at all. My brothers refuse to take my mom and my dad only goes if she promises to cook his favorite dinner."

"I know, he told me. So, tomorrow night, my mom is making spaghetti for us."

Dana laughed again and extricated herself from Bruno's arms. "I'll get my coat."

"You have to take her to Sunflower or wherever she wants to go to buy the ingredients."

"Where is she going to cook?"

"My kitchen now meets her high standards so we'll have dinner at my place."

Dana breathed a sigh of relief. Having Angelina in her kitchen, passing judgment on it would be unnerving.

"Hi, Mrs. Bruno," Dana said as she slipped into the car.

"Oh, no," Angelina told her. "It's Angie. I told you that last time. After the wedding, then you call me Mama."

Bruno closed the door and walked around to the driver's side of the car. Through the windshield, Dana could see him smiling.

"Okay, Angie. How was your shopping trip?"

"I found a nice dress. I hope you like it. Bruno said it

makes me look thin. That's why I bought it, but I think he was lying just to get me out of the store."

"It was the twenty-fifth store we'd been in, Mama," Bruno said defensively.

"Well, we'll see what Dana thinks of the dress. If she doesn't like it, you will take me back tomorrow to buy a different dress."

"I have to work tomorrow," Bruno told her. "And Dana is taking you shopping for groceries."

"Oh, yes, Dana," Angie said. "My son had to be bribed to take his mama shopping. All the years I had to take him shopping for clothes in the chubby departments."

"It wasn't chubby, it was husky," Bruno protested.

"He got the idea for the bribe from my father," Dana said.

The three of them bantered back and forth all the way to the Ventana. No matter what Bruno said, his mother had an answer for him and Dana was enjoying it.

"Such a beautiful place," Angie said when they pulled up in front of the hotel. "I hope my dress is suitable."

The valet helped Dana out while Bruno got his mother out of the backseat. Then, walking between Dana and his mother, Bruno escorted them into the hotel.

The lobby of the new hotel was all crystal and gold with a fountain in the middle of it. There was a sign on a easel that directed them to the ballroom where the charity dinner was being held.

Just outside the door of the ballroom they checked their coats. Bruno was wearing his devastating brown suit again and his mother, who was a little on the plump side, did look thinner in a two-piece silk dress. It was a lovely purple sheath with a short orchard jacket with purple piping around the collar and sleeves. Her black hair was streaked with silver and cut short in a style that was very becoming.

She had used makeup to emphasize her dark eyes and bring color to her cheeks.

"You look amazing," Dana told her as they hugged. "I love your new hairstyle."

"I had a makeover. My daughters thought I looked dowdy so they chipped in and took me to a spa. I liked it, so now I go every month."

Dana laughed. "That's wonderful."

With their coats all checked, Bruno escorted them into the ballroom. Marianne and Greg were already seated at a table for six and waved them over.

Bruno introduced his mother to Greg and Marianne. Greg stood politely until Bruno had helped his mother and Dana into their chairs.

Marianne looked stunning in an emerald green silk pantsuit that matched her eyes. Greg was tall and broad-shouldered. He wasn't what would be called handsome, but he had a nice face and an easygoing manner. Tonight he looked very good in a black pinstriped suit with a white shirt and a black tie.

Once everyone was seated, a waiter came around and poured champagne into their glasses.

"I like the bubbles," Angie announced. "It's a happy drink."

Everyone laughed and they toasted one another. For a charity event the dinner was surprisingly good. After dinner there were speakers interspersed with music from an excellent trio.

In between that Angelina kept them all entertained with stories of her grandchildren, her work as a volunteer at a shelter and gossip from the Bingo hall.

Toward the end of the evening, Lucille came by with her husband in tow and greeted all the people who had purchased tickets from her and thanked them for coming.

"This is a wonderful thing you have done here tonight," Angie told Lou. "Bringing all these people together to help the children. God Bless."

"I've just been told that we have reached our goal and they'll start expanding the children's wing as soon as the ground thaws. They'll be announcing the details soon," Lou told them softly. "Act surprised."

"Do they have many weddings in this ballroom?" Angie asked suddenly.

"The hotel just opened a few months ago," Dana told her. "But I'm sure there will be many weddings held here, especially in the summertime when the garden is in bloom."

Angie turned to Bruno. "Maybe you should reserve your date now."

"For what?" he asked, feigning ignorance.

"For your wedding, of course."

"She hasn't said yes yet," Bruno reminded her.

"She will. Won't you, Dana?"

Dana felt the color rise in her cheeks. "That's a possibility," she said, then quickly picked up her champagne glass and took a long sip.

Angie just smiled knowingly and turned her attention to Marianne and Greg. "And what about you two? I can see the promise of bambinos in those lovely green eyes. When will you marry?"

Marianne looked at Dana for help, but Dana was studying the crystal chandelier, still sipping her champagne.

"As soon as I'm more settled in my career," Greg answered. "I'm not in a position to support a wife as yet."

Angie shook her head. "You young people, always want everything perfect before you marry these days. Life does not work that way. If you wait until everything is perfect, you will be so old, you will need assistance to walk down the aisle."

"I've already got my walker reserved," Bruno said. "Come on, Mama. There are some people I want you to meet."

Bruno pulled out her chair and took her off to meet some of the city councilmen who were seated a few tables away.

"You were right, Dana," Marianne said when they were out of earshot. "She's quite a character. Now I know who Bruno takes after."

"She scares me," Greg said. "Maybe we'd better get engaged before she comes back."

TWENTY-EIGHT

THE NEXT MORNING, Dana woke up with an idea that must have surfaced while she was sleeping. It was a sudden melding of information. A man wearing an Arizona Cardinals hat had been seen in the pool hall the night Lucas Porter died and someone with a similar hat had been seen going up to John Hunter's apartment. The bank manager that had been engaged to Sarah Turner had moved to Arizona after the trial. It was the kind of idea that would keep nagging at her all day if she didn't check into it immediately.

Bruno had to work and she was in charge of entertaining his mother. They were having an early lunch at Rose Marie's Tea Room and then going shopping for groceries so Angie could make her famous spaghetti sauce.

Before they parted the night before, Angie had invited Greg and Marianne to have dinner with them and since Bruno's apartment was too small to accommodate six people for dinner, they were now going to have dinner at Dana's apartment.

Dana called the office and Marianne answered. "I've got an off-the-wall idea," she said. "Can you look on your computer and see what the requirements are to sell real estate in Arizona? I know that some states require agents to be fingerprinted and I need to know if Arizona is one of them."

"Sure. Hold on," Marianne said.

Within a few minutes, she came back on the line. "Arizona

does require all agents to be fingerprinted before issuing licenses to them."

"Good. Now I'll have to beg Bruno for a favor."

"And I thought you would just enjoy your day off," Marianne said.

"I will if I can talk Bruno into cooperating."

Marianne laughed. "If he doesn't do it, threaten to tell his mother."

"Good idea."

"I'll see you for dinner tonight. Are you sure I can't bring something?"

"Just Greg."

"Okay."

Dana poured herself a cup of coffee and dialed Bruno's direct number at the station. "Homicide, Detective O'Brien."

Dana hung up on him and dialed Bruno's cell phone. "Did you ditch my mama already?" he said when he answered.

"We're going to lunch at eleven and then I'll take her grocery shopping. They're predicting snow for this afternoon so I want to get the running around done early. Where are you?"

"I'm on my way to talk to Tony Hunter's ex-girlfriend. One of his golfing buddies gave me her name but she's been out of town until yesterday."

"I need you to do me a favor," Dana said.

"Here we go again."

Ignoring his sarcasm, Dana continued. "Can your lab guys access any fingerprint databases in Arizona?"

"It depends."

"I did some checking and found out that real estate agents in Arizona have to be fingerprinted. That's the database I want the lab to run that fingerprint on the anonymous letter through."

"Why?"

"Just an idea I woke up with this morning. Will you ask them to do that, please?"

"Who are you hoping it will belong to?"

"Stuart Hollingsworth."

"Who's he?"

"Bruno, can you please just ask the lab to do it as soon as possible. If it turns out to be Hollingsworth, I'll give you all the information I've gathered on him."

"Why can't you tell me now?"

"Because I'm picking your mother up for lunch at eleven and I have to shower and get dressed."

"It's only eight-thirty."

"Should I call Troy Kimball and ask him to get it done?"

"I think you've communicated with Kimball quite enough, sweetheart. Louis says his case has weakened thanks to you."

"I'm only trying to get at the truth," Dana said impatiently. "Are you going to call in a favor at the lab for me or not?"

"I'll do it, but if your hunch is wrong, you'll have to make it up to me."

"I will. Thanks. I've got to go. Love you," Dana said all in one breath and then clicked off the phone.

Lunch at Rose Marie's Tea Room was lovely. Angie was full of questions about Dana's parents and seemed excited by the prospect of going to the farm to meet them.

"I just hope the weather cooperates," Dana said. "Although if the roads get iced over, we may still be able to go down on the train. I do that sometimes."

"Is your mother expecting us at a certain time?"

"No. I just said I'd give her a few hours' notice. My mother always has an abundance of food in the freezer and can whip up a dinner in the blink of an eye."

"Al said she is a very good cook. Does she make much pasta?"

"Very seldom and it can't compare to yours. Bruno says your recipe is so secret it's locked in a vault."

Angie laughed. "Today you will help me prepare the sauce and you will learn the secrets."

"Really?" Dana was both surprised and flattered. "I'd love that."

"Good. My daughters never wanted to learn and someone in the family has to know how to do it."

Dana smiled at her. Every chance she got, Angie put in a plug for Dana and Bruno to marry. Dana was getting used to it, and had to admit the way she took their eventual union for granted was like she was giving Dana her stamp of approval as a future daughter-in-law.

They finished lunch and Angie went to the ladies' room while Dana took care of the bill. As she collected her change, her cell phone rang.

"Hi, sweets," Bruno said. "How was lunch?"

"Very nice. How did your interview go?"

"I didn't learn much. The girlfriend claims she only dated Hunter a few times and thought he was too weird and secretive, so she stopped seeing him."

"If only Casey had done the same," Dana said.

"I agree, but the reason I'm calling is to tell you that your hunch was right on. The fingerprint matched up with an Arizona real estate agent named Stuart G. Hollingsworth. Now who is he and which one of my cases is he involved in?"

"He was engaged to Sarah Turner and was the assistant

manager of the bank the Hunter brothers robbed. His name turned up in the trial transcripts." Angie returned to Dana's side. "Your mom and I are leaving now to do the grocery shopping. I'll tell you everything I know later, but see if you can trace this guy's whereabouts now. I think he may be important."

Angie realized that Dana was talking to her son and wanted to say hello. She told him that she was going to teach Dana how to make her spaghetti sauce. "She will watch and write down what I do," Angie said. "The recipe is in my head." Angie said good-bye to Bruno and turned to Dana. "My son is speechless."

Dana laughed and they hurried out the door to the car. It was starting to snow and the flakes were big and wet.

The streets were starting to get coated with the new fallen snow, so Dana had to drive with extra caution. She decided to shop at the Sunflower Market because it was on the way to her apartment.

The parking lot was crowded so Dana had to park down at the end in front of a vacant store. The empty store had been a pet shop that had moved to a bigger location a few months earlier. Dana had once fallen in love with a darling puppy in their window, but had decided against buying him because she wasn't home enough to take proper care of a dog.

Since Angie was not familiar with the layout of the market and Dana usually only came in there to pick up things from the deli, their shopping took longer than expected.

As they made their way down the aisles, they encountered the store manager. Ron Morgan remembered Dana and greeted her. She introduced him to Angie and then they continued on their way.

"We must get fresh garlic and onions from the produce section," Angie said absently. "What about ensalada?"

"We need that too," Dana replied.

When they got to the produce department, Dana went to the lettuce bin to search for a firm head, leaving Angie to choose a proper onion.

Dana turned around when she heard Angie shout. "George! I don't believe it. What are you doing here?"

Bruno's mom had George trapped in one of her enthusiastic hugs. Dana hurried over to them.

"I assume you two know each other?"

"Of course. We used to live next door to each other in the old neighborhood," Angie said, letting go of George who looked very confused. "George, meet my future daughter-in-law, Dana Sloan. Dana, this is George Hollingsworth."

Dana was stunned, but tried to hide it. "George and I know each other, Angie. He's the most helpful person in the store."

"George," Angie said. "I haven't seen you since your father's funeral. You were living in Arizona then."

"That was a long time ago. I'm surprised you recognized me."

"You look just like your father, God rest his soul. That's how I knew it was you.'

George nodded. "Right. So, how have you been?"

"Very good. Listen, I'm cooking dinner tonight and you should come." She turned to Dana. "We can fit one more?"

"Of course," Dana said, wondering if George was related to Stuart Hollingsworth.

"Oh, thank you, but I can't. I have other plans."

"Well, I'll be in town for a week. We must get together. Give me your number and I'll call you."

"I don't have a phone, Mrs. Bruno, but you can call me here at the store. I'm sure Miss Sloan has the number."

"Yes, I do."

"Good. I'll call you and we'll have lunch or dinner and catch up," Angie said. "What a wonderful thing to run into you like this. Wait until I tell my son. He's a homicide detective here in Crescent Hills, you know."

"No, I didn't know that," George replied. Although Angie didn't seem to notice, his discomfort was obvious.

"We'd better get going, Angie," Dana said. "The snow is getting worse."

Within a few minutes, Angie and Dana were in the checkout line. "George Hollingsworth is from Chicago?" Dana said trying to sound casual. "Do you know if he's related to a man named Stuart Hollingsworth?"

"He is Stuart Hollingsworth, but his father was also Stuart so we always called the son by his middle name, George."

"I see," Dana said slowly as she remembered the bank manager's name in the court transcripts was Stuart G. Hollingsworth. She would have pulled out her cell phone and called Bruno immediately, but she didn't want to upset Angie by letting her know that her long-lost friend was a suspect in a homicide.

With their groceries bagged and stacked in the grocery cart, Angie and Dana left the store. Dana pushed the cart down the sidewalk toward the far end of the parking lot where her blue Mustang was parked.

"You'd better hold on to the cart, Angie," Dana said. "This walkway is getting slippery."

"It is snowing harder, soon the streets may be a mess."

"It's okay, we're heading home now to start cooking," Dana said.

Dana had her cell phone in her hand. She was trying to decide if she should call Bruno as soon as she got into the car, or wait until she got home so she could find a way to speak to him privately about Hollingsworth.

While he could be perfectly innocent, the fact that he had lived in the state of Arizona where the Cardinals played, had sent an anonymous letter to the paper claiming to have killed Lucas Porter and had a motive to kill both Tony and John Hunter was too much to ignore. The man had to be picked up and questioned.

Dana opened the trunk of her car and she and Angie started loading the groceries inside. They had the bags all stacked neatly inside when George Hollingsworth came out of the empty store and approached them.

"Close the trunk and move away from it," he said softly. "Don't make me shoot you."

TWENTY-NINE

BRUNO STOMPED UP the stairs to Dana's apartment expecting to discover the wonderful aroma of his mother's spaghetti sauce permeating the hallway. He had finished up at the station a little early and had come over to see if he could help his two favorite women with dinner.

He rang the doorbell insistently like he always did, but the apartment was quiet and no one came to the door. He rang the bell a few more times and knocked as well, still no answer.

Thinking maybe they were in the kitchen at the back of the apartment and couldn't hear him at the door, Bruno trudged down the stairs again.

The snow was already a few inches deep so Bruno walked carefully around the building to the back and climbed those stairs. The back windows were covered with wrought-iron security bars and Dana had hung some heavy curtains over the windows to hide them so Bruno couldn't see inside the kitchen. However, he could tell that there were no lights on in the apartment.

Bruno pulled out his cell phone and dialed Dana's cell number. He got an out-of-service signal, so he clicked off and dialed her home number. He could hear the phone ringing from inside her apartment and listened to it ring five times before he got the answering device.

"Where are they?" he mumbled to himself as he went back down the stairs to the front of the building again.

He went inside the building and sat down on the stairs as he dialed Globe Investigations. Marianne answered.

"Hi, Marianne, it's Bruno. Is Dana there?"

"No. She took the day off to be with your mother."

"I know that, but I'm at Dana's apartment and they're not here."

"Is her car there?" Marianne asked.

Bruno looked outside the glass door at Dana's usual parking space. It was empty. "No. It's not here," he told Marianne. "And I tried her cell and got an out of service message."

"That's odd," Marianne said. "Maybe they got stuck in the snow someplace."

DANA AND ANGIE were not stuck in the snow. They were stuck in Dana's car with George Hollingsworth. Dana was driving and Angie was buckled into the passenger's seat. George was in the backseat, holding a gun to the back of Angie's head.

Angie had been asking George a lot of questions that he refused to answer. He finally told her to shut up or he'd blow her head off.

"Where are you taking us?" she asked without so much as a quiver in her voice.

"Out of town," he replied. "Now shut up. You always did talk too much."

"Don't you want to tell us how you killed the Hunter brothers?" Dana said evenly.

"The Hunter brothers," Angie said before George could answer. "Those were the young men who held up your bank and killed your Sarah."

"That's right, Angie. I've been waiting all these years to get justice. I was hoping they'd die in prison. Sarah's father told me he was going to hire someone on the inside to kill them. He had connections to the Mob, but I guess his connections weren't good enough because it never happened."

"I can't believe it. You were always such a nice boy."

George laughed. "Not as nice as you think."

"That's right," Dana said. "George and Sarah planned the robbery. They used the Hunter boys to pull it off and then they were going to get the money from them and take off with it."

"Who told you that?" George asked.

"Mary Lou Bandini."

"Mary Lou told you," Angie said incredulously. "She's in jail for embezzling money from the nursing home where she worked. Everyone in the neighborhood was shocked. How did you talk to her?"

"I went to the correctional facility where she's being held and visited her last week."

"Some things never change," George said cynically. "Mary Lou always had a big mouth. Did she tell you that she was the one who turned in John and Tony?"

"Yes. She said she did it because they killed her friend, Sarah."

"She probably did it hoping to get her greedy little hands on the bank money, but the Hunter boys turned out to be smarter than anyone gave them credit for. They killed Sarah when she tried to take off with the cash and then they hid it so well no one ever found it."

"Is that why you didn't kill Tony as soon as he turned up in Crescent Hills?" Dana asked. "Were you hoping he'd lead you to the money?"

"No. I didn't kill him right away because I knew that if he got out of jail, his brother would soon follow and I wanted to take care of them both at the same time."

"Then you found out that Tony married Casey and you acted immediately."

"I went to his place hoping she'd be there. The plan was to kill her first in front of Tony. I wanted him to know how it feels to lose someone you love. Only when I got there she was gone. Tony said they had some kind of an argument and he threw her out. That's when I shot him."

Dana took a deep breath, stunned at how close her friend had come to being murdered. "Casey was innocent. She didn't know anything about Tony's past."

"Okay," Angie said in a firm voice. "So, you killed some bad people, but why are you doing this to us? We are good people."

"Your friend here is an investigator, a very smart investigator. I knew when I saw you together this afternoon, you'd tell her all about me and how I was a bank manager and how my fiancée was murdered by the Hunter brothers. She's been investigating the case here and she was in Chicago when I killed Johnny boy. I'm sure my name must have popped up somewhere judging from the look on her face when you blurted it out earlier. Then of course you threw in that little tidbit about your son being a homicide detective and her boyfriend to boot."

"You came from a nice family, George. They would be so ashamed," Angie told him.

"The roads are getting very slippery," Dana said. "I'm going to have to slow down."

"And give your boyfriend a chance to catch up with us. I don't think so. Pull over to the side of the road. This is where you two get out."

"Get out?" Angie said. "We're in the middle of nowhere."

"That's the idea," George told her.

Dana pulled the car off to the side. The road they were

on was deserted. There was no one to see them. George had taken her cell phone and crushed it under his foot before they got into the car. Dana could only hope that the weapon she had managed to slip into her coat pocket would be enough to save them.

BRUNO WAS BESIDE HIMSELF with worry. He had put out an APB on Dana's car, but so far nothing had been reported. He had decided to try and retrace their steps.

The last time he talked to Dana she had said they were going grocery shopping. With the snow, he was hoping she had decided to shop at the Sunflower Market as that was on the way to her apartment and he knew she liked the store.

Marianne and Greg were at Dana's apartment. Fortunately, Dana kept an extra set of keys at the office. Bruno and Dana used to have keys to each other's apartments, but the last time they had a big argument, Dana had changed her locks and refused to give him a key to it.

"Where's the manager?" Bruno asked the woman at the nearest cash register.

"Who wants to know?" she asked.

Bruno flashed his badge and she said she'd page him. Ron Morgan answered the page within a few minutes and Bruno suggested that they go back to his office to talk.

"I need to know if my mother and Dana Sloan were in here shopping earlier," Bruno said as soon as they got inside Morgan's office.

"Yes, they were. I spoke to them. Is something wrong?"

"They've disappeared."

"This must be the day for that."

"Pardon me?"

"One of my employees is also missing. One minute he was in the produce department replenishing the vegetables and the next minute he was gone. No one seems to know where he went."

"What's his name?"

"George Hollingsworth."

The name immediately registered and Bruno felt a prickle of fear run down his spine. "Is he related to a Stuart Hollingsworth?"

"I'll check." Morgan opened a file cabinet behind him and pulled out a personnel file. He looked at it briefly. "His first name is Stuart, but he goes by his middle name, which is George."

"Come outside with me and see if his car is in the parking lot. I know Dana's car isn't there because I've already looked."

Morgan got his jacket and followed Bruno outside. "The employees park down at the end by that empty store." Bruno and Morgan hurried down to the end of the walkway. "That's George's car there, the white Nissan."

As Bruno stepped off the curb to get a closer look at the white car, he stepped on something and had to grab on to another parked car to keep from sliding off his feet.

He bent down and picked up Dana's phone that had been smashed and left in the parking lot to be covered with snow.

"Where does this guy live?" Bruno asked, trying not to panic.

"I don't know, but I'm sure his address is in his file."

"Let's go get it."

THE MILD-MANNERED, jovial man Dana knew as George had turned into a cold-blooded killer. He ordered Dana to leave the car running and get out. Then, still holding the gun to Angie's head, he ordered her out of the car and quickly got out himself, so he could keep the gun leveled at her.

"Are you going to shoot us with that gun?" Angie asked as they stumbled across the snow-covered ground toward a wooded area away from the road.

"Shut up, Angie," George said firmly. "Who wants to die first?"

"I do," Dana said. "But first I have to know something."

"Your last wish?" he asked coldly.

"I understand why you murdered the Hunter brothers but why did you kill Lucas Porter and then send that anonymous letter to the paper?"

"Lucas Porter was practice."

"Practice," Dana repeated. "I don't get it."

"Lucas was a scumbag. He beat up on that pretty little wife of his so I decided to practice on him. You see, as Angie pointed out, I was always a nice guy. I'd never killed anyone before and I wanted to make sure I could do it before I faced the Hunter brothers. I thought beating him to death was appropriate after the way he battered his wife. I knew if I could do that, the Hunter boys would be easy. I sent the letter because I felt badly that the wife and her little friend were getting blamed for it."

"You left a fingerprint on the letter and it was matched to the fingerprints on file with the real estate commission in Arizona."

"See, Angie. What did I tell you? This gal is real smart."

"Listen, George," Angie said, edging closer to him. "You don't have to kill us. Just leave us and we'll freeze to death out here in the snow."

"That's right, George," Dana said picking up Angie's lead. "No one comes down this road and if that is the same gun you used to kill Tony and John with, when they find our bodies they'll know you killed us and Bruno will not rest until he tracks you down."

"He'll never find me. My escape route is all planned out. Sending that letter was a mistake, and not leaving town sooner was another, but I can't go back and change that."

Dana looked around. The snow was getting very deep. If they tried to run, they wouldn't get very far. George grabbed Angie's arm and pulled her close to him. He placed the gun at her temple.

"Say good-bye, old girl," he said.

A SEARCH OF GEORGE'S apartment didn't yield any clues, except an Arizona Cardinals hat. Bruno was beginning to panic. He got back in his car and drove to the Sunflower parking lot again and then drove past it to the road that led out of town.

It was obvious that they had left in Dana's Mustang. The problem was that Bruno didn't know if they had driven out on the road that led out of town toward the country or had gotten on the expressway and headed toward Chicago.

The planes at O'Hare and Midway were grounded because of the weather, and Bruno had stationed men at the Crescent Hills train station and bus depot. However, there was no way of covering the Chicago stations and bus terminals.

As Bruno drove slowly down the road looking left and right for a sign of Dana's car, he began to pray. He was a man who dealt with violence and murder on a regular basis and he had learned to detach himself from the crime scenes and the victims. This was different. These were the two people he loved most in the world. If he lost them, he didn't know how he would survive.

George Hollingsworth had lost the woman he loved and had waited almost twenty-five years to avenge her death. The pain Bruno felt now must have been what Hollingsworth had felt when the Hunter brothers killed his fiancée.

Suddenly Bruno noticed car tracks on the side of the road. A car had pulled off the road there. He stopped his vehicle and got out his flashlight to take a look.

There were lots of footprints and signs of a struggle there in the snow. Then, his light shone on a dark patch that stood out dramatically on the white frost that covered the ground. It was blood. A trail of it started at the edge of the woods and led back to the road.

Bruno stared at the bloody trail as a numbness crept over him. He went back to his car to radio for help to search the area.

As he reached for the radio, his cell phone rang. "Hello," he managed to say when he answered it.

"Bruno, it's Jack. Your girlfriend and your mother just showed up here."

"What? Are they all right?"

"Yeah, they're fine, but the guy they got stuffed in the trunk of the car doesn't look so hot."

THIRTY

DESPITE THE ICY ROADS and streets, Bruno made it back to the station in under thirty minutes. Putting the emergency flasher and siren on helped him navigate what little traffic was still on the streets.

He double-parked in front of the station next to Dana's Mustang. As he passed by it, he saw bags of groceries on the backseat.

Bruno bounded up the steps and pushed through the door, letting in a blast of cold air. "Where are they?" he yelled to the desk sergeant.

"Interview room two," he yelled back. "They're expecting you."

As he ran down the hallway to room two, Bruno heard a burst of laughter. The room was soundproof, but the door was standing open and Jack O'Brien was in the doorway laughing so hard he was crying.

Bruno yanked him out of the way and crashed into the room. Dana and Angie were sitting at the interview table. Besides Jack, there were two uniformed cops in the room. Everyone stopped laughing and turned to look at Bruno.

Dana and Angie both got up and ran into his arms. Tears of relief were streaming down his face. "My God," he whispered. "I thought I'd lost you both."

"Dana saved my life," Angie told him.

"No," Dana protested. "Angie gets the credit."

Jack and the other officers had the good sense to leave

the room. After a few minutes, Bruno calmed down and was able to release them from his suffocating embrace.

Dana and Angie sat down again and Bruno threw off his coat and sat down across from them. He stared at their faces, so beautiful, so alive.

"What happened?" he finally asked.

"Has anyone filled you in on Hollingsworth?" Dana asked.

"Marianne did. Then I went to Sunflower and found out he worked there and had disappeared at the same time you did. I also found your cell phone smashed in the parking lot."

"Right," Dana said. "It turned out that your mother knows George and told me his last name. I was unable to hide my surprise and he realized that I had connected him to the murders."

"Wait a minute." Bruno held up his hand. "My mother knows this murderer?"

"We grew up in the same neighborhood," Angie said defensively. "He wasn't a murderer then, but I knew about the robbery and his girlfriend being killed and he knew I would tell Dana so he came after us. Oh, and I also happened to mention that my son was a homicide detective."

"I was just about to call you when he came out of the vacant store and put a gun to our heads."

"We were putting the groceries in the trunk," Angie added. "I saw Dana grab a can of tomato paste and slip it into her pocket. So, I grabbed a can too. George was too busy smashing Dana's cell phone and waving his gun around to notice."

"He made us drive out into the country and pull off the road," Dana continued. "He was going to shoot us both and drive off in my car. He grabbed Angie first and put the gun to her head. I pulled out the can of tomato paste and threw it as hard as I could. It hit him in the face and threw him off balance. He dropped the gun and as he dove for it, your mother took out a can of jumbo olives and knocked him out cold."

"I saw where you pulled off the road. There was a lot of blood," Bruno told them.

"George's," his mother said. "They took him to the hospital. I think he has a concussion."

"Maybe a fractured skull," Dana added. "Anyway, I got the gun and held it on him but he was unconscious. We opened the trunk, transferred the groceries to the backseat and then the two of us picked up George and dragged him to the car and managed to lock him in the trunk."

"Then Dana turned the car around and we drove straight to the police station. And here we are. Good thing it's so cold outside, it will keep the groceries from spoiling."

Bruno looked at the two of them in disbelief. "So George the friendly grocer you are always talking about killed Tony Hunter."

"And John Hunter and Lucas Porter. Remember his fingerprint on the anonymous letter is what made it all fit together."

"Marianne told me he sold real estate in Arizona where they have to be fingerprinted and that's where he became an Arizona Cardinals fan. Louis told me about the witness Bob found and about the salesman at the hardware store who sold him the hammer. Why did he kill Porter?"

"Practice!" Dana and Angie said at the same time. Then they looked at each other and hugged.

DANA AND ANGIE's ordeal made the front page the next morning, with Dana's byline, of course.

The spaghetti dinner took place that night with Casey as an additional guest. As Angie said, the cold air kept the groceries from spoiling. Dana was allowed to assist with the sauce, but mostly she just watched Angie and wrote down everything she did. When Angie started to add a half-handful of sugar to the bubbling mixture, Dana made her stop, got the measuring spoons and figured out how much that was. Angie was delighted to have someone so interested in her secret recipe.

Once the sauce was simmering, Dana took Casey into the bedroom for a private talk. She told her that the master plan had actually saved her life. If Tony hadn't become so angry about it and pushed her out of the apartment, George would have shot her too.

"I can't believe it," Casey said. "George was such a sweetheart."

Stuart G. Hollingsworth was still in the hospital recovering from his head wound. The police had the gun he used to kill Tony and John, so George confessed to everything, thereby closing three homicide cases and forcing Louis Hildago to drop all the charges against Judy Porter and Teddy Larson.

The spaghetti dinner was fabulous and everyone had a good time. Even Casey seemed to have fun, a sign that she was going to be her old self again.

Early Sunday morning, Bruno, Dana and Angie drove to the Sloan farm. There in the country, the snow was knee-deep and perfect for snowball fights and building snowmen. Several frosty characters were constructed with Bruno and Dana's brothers supervising the little ones.

The women were all gathered in the kitchen. Linda and Angelina were getting along like soul mates. Dana decided to slip away to the den to visit with her dad.

Warren Sloan was sitting by the window watching the men and the kids making the most of the winter wonderland.

Dana came over and perched on the arm of the chair,

kissing her dad on top of his bald head. "It's good to be home," she said.

"From what I read in the paper, you and Angie had a very close call. When are you going to stop being a lady gang-buster and settle down, daughter?" her dad asked.

"You've been talking to Bruno again," Dana said.

"Yes. You two scared him so bad, he's thinking about quitting the force."

"He always says that, but he doesn't mean it."

"I think he'd do it in a heartbeat if he thought it would keep you safe."

"I don't do what I do because Bruno is a cop," Dana said. "I was doing it before I met him."

"And you're going to keep on doing it?"

"Yes. My staff and I help a lot of people."

"Okay," he agreed. "As long as you're happy."

Dana gazed out the window at Bruno. The little ones were all chasing him with snowballs in their hands. Bruno ran in a circle for a few minutes and then let the kids catch him. They howled with laughter when he fell to the ground and they were able to cover him with snow.

"Remember the bambinos," Dana said softly.

"What was that?" her dad asked.

"A promise that's part of my master plan," she replied with a distant smile.

REQUEST YOUR FREE BOOKS!

2 FREE NOVELS
PLUS 2 FREE GIFTS!

Your Partner in Crime